BIG AND BAD

Anna K. Scotti

# BiG AND BAD

A Novella

**Texas Review Press**
HUNTSVILLE • TEXAS

Library of Congress Cataloging in Publication Data
Names: Scotti, Anna K., author.
Title: Big and bad : a novella / Anna K. Scotti.
Description: Huntsville, Texas : Texas Review Press, [2020]
Identifiers: LCCN 2019052025 (print) | LCCN 2019052026 (ebook) | ISBN
    9781680031966 (paperback) | ISBN 9781680032055 (ebook)
Subjects: LCSH: Teenage girls—California—Fiction. |
    Families—California—Fiction. | Dogs—Fiction. | Problem
    youth—Fiction. | Friendship—Fiction. | Teenage girls—Family
    relationships—Fiction. | Motherless families—Fiction. |
    Dogfighting—California—Fiction. | LCGFT: Novellas.
Classification: LCC PS3619.C6965 B54 2020  (print) | LCC PS3619.C6965
    (ebook) | DDC 813/.6—dc23
LC record available at https://lccn.loc.gov/2019052025
LC ebook record available at https://lccn.loc.gov/2019052026

Cover photo courtesy Victoria Scotti, 2019

*for my students, past and present, dog lovers all,
and for Daisy, Charlie, Baron, Banzai, and Lady*

## CHAPTER ONE

# Candy Is Dandy, Sort of

The first time my dad brought the dog home it had been raining for three days straight. People think it never rains in Southern California, but that's a myth. It even snows, up in the mountains, but down here in the flats it just rains — for weeks, sometimes, in winter — dawn after dawn of gloomy cold, the damp seeping through your clothes and into your bones. It's never quite enough to bother with putting up an umbrella, and anyway, when it rains, the wind blows, so you'd just end up with this cold spray wetting your body while you struggled with an umbrella getting yanked out of your hands or turned inside out.

When Dad pulled up in his battered Ford Ranger, I was sitting by my window, watching the street. There was this new kid hanging around, the building manager's nephew or cousin, I guessed, even though he never seemed to do much by way of helping — I'd see Rafael lugging out three or four big Hefty bags of garbage, and the kid'd be lounging on the front stoop with a book, barely looking up when Rafael passed by. I'd seen him coming up the block late at night, wearing some kind of stupid cap like they make you wear at a fast food place, and even then he'd have some book tucked under his arm. He had a key to let himself into the little ground floor apartment where Rafael and Luisa and their kids live. I will admit, I was sort of watching for him when my dad pulled up.

I knew whatever plans my dad had for that dog were not going to be happy ones. The way he yanked the chain, dragging the dog down the basement steps without even giving it a chance to go willingly, said it all. That dog clearly would have preferred to slip free and disappear into the wet night. He was a big shaggy shepherd with biscuit-colored fur and muscular hind legs, though he seemed thin beneath the padding of his coat. He had a red leather collar around his neck, the kind with silver studs on it that are supposed to look tough. He was as big as a rottie, at least, but he didn't have that thick, blunt biter face. His muzzle was kind of tapered, and his ears hung down in soft ragged flaps. I thought he was an Aussie or some breed like that.

My dad cursed and yanked the rope again and the dog rolled his eyes up in his head, and for a second it was like he was looking at me. Then he stumbled, tripping over his own big front paws and tumbling out of sight, down the steps into the dark hole of our basement where nobody but Dad or Rafael ever went willingly.

When we moved here, Mom promised it was just for a short time; she said we'd look for something better soon as Dad got a better job. That stuff never happens the way parents plan, but you've gotta feel sorry for them, the way they fall for their own stories, time after time, all starry-eyed like princesses in a Disney movie. Everything's always "next week" or "next month" or "when times get a little better." But I didn't mind so much. I had my own room and an unlimited supply of roach motels from the 99 Cents Only store where my mom found a temp job—*just till Dad gets something better*—and I didn't really mind changing schools again, since the one I'd been going to hadn't exactly worked out. Ahem. What did worry me was Mom's endless cough—no amount of cough syrup seemed to help for long, and the one time she got it together and went down to the clinic, they told her she needed to take antibiotics, which she did, since they gave them free, and then to come back for an X-ray in a month or so, which she didn't, because by then she was dead.

Yeah.

Nobody did anything wrong, despite my dad's ranting about suing and malpractice and shitty health care and everything else. He's probably right about the health care—we didn't any of us have insurance—but I don't think the doctors were to blame. Mom had some kind of infection in her lungs, which they gave her medicine for, and the rest of it—the fever, the tiredness—would have gotten better if she'd been able to rest, and eat right, and quit smoking. Which she didn't do, the quitting smoking part, until the very end when it was actually too late. She was sick a long time, but not very sick. And then one morning she spiked a high fever—my dad hauled ass down the street for a thermometer, and by the time he got back I'd cooled her off with Tylenol and wet cloths, and it *still* registered 104. Then Dad jammed. He wrapped Mom up in a blanket and carried her down the steps like she weighed nothing, and all the while she was coughing and choking and couldn't get her breath. I'd already called 911, as soon as I saw those digital bars on the thermometer switching side-top-side-bottom to make new numbers, higher numbers, really fast, way too fast, and by the time Dad got Mom downstairs and onto the front stoop, the paramedics were there, opening the back of the gleaming white ambulance truck. One of them was saying something, and the other stifled a laugh as he looked up and saw us barging out the front door.

You can't blame them—they weren't laughing at us. They were doing their job, which to them is no different from the job of a doctor or lawyer or pizza delivery person, and those guys get to chat and mess around and laugh on the job, so why not an ambulance driver? But Dad held that against them too.

"She's a hunnerd and five," he yelled, even in his panic not neglecting to dramatize. Mom's hand fell out of the blanket then, and it shocked me how white it was, how lifeless, despite her low steady panting and the sweat that glistened on her pale forehead.

The pink-skinned ambulance man snapped open this little traveling stretcher thing, one-two-three, and then they were bundling Mom down the steps, and believe me, nobody was laughing then. Those guys were all business. Stretcher guy unwrapped Mom right there, right in plain sight on the sidewalk, and Dad tried to pull her T-shirt down over her underpants and her trembling bare legs, but the brown-skinned paramedic brushed him away, bending low over Mom with a stethoscope, holding her wrist, touching her throat, her chest, her stomach . . .

"She needs the hospital," Dad said helplessly. "She's sick bad. She's coughing. There's blood on the Kleenex. There's—"

"Step back, sir," stethoscope guy said crisply, and I was able to really see him, then, his clean dark skin against the blinding white of his uniform, and I thought how his truck and his uniform made him look like an ice cream man. How good an ice cream would have been then, beneath the blazing orange sun.

My dad was frantic, pacing up and down the sidewalk, waving his hands, glancing from the ambulance to the apartment to me, sitting like a dull stupid lump on our front step, watching the whole thing like it wasn't about me, about my family, about my mom. Like it wasn't the last time I'd see her alive, like it wasn't my last chance to tell her that I loved her, that I liked the purple jelly sandals she'd bought for me on sale at Payless, that I forgave her for not being rich and pretty and for not having a soft pretty voice like the moms in TV commercials, that I needed her still, needed her desperately, even though I usually forgot her birthday, and sometimes didn't even bother to look up from my book when she came into the room. I sat there thinking about ice cream and the weather and how the heat was so thick and hot it was almost like being at the bottom of a deep, warm swimming pool, it was that surrounding and nearly that hard to breathe. I didn't think about it being the last time I would see my mom alive.

But it was.

## CHAPTER TWO

# But the Cupboard Was Bare

"Candy!" Dad yelled, and I jerked awake, legs swinging up and out of bed and onto the cold floor before my eyes were even fully open. I pushed my hair back out of my face and reached for my jeans. I'd slept in a T-shirt and it would have to do for now—when my dad hollered, he wanted an immediate response, no matter if you were sleeping, on the phone—or even in the bathroom.

I stumbled down the hall into the kitchen. Dad was chugging coffee over the sink. When he finished, he set his cup on top of the pile of unwashed dishes. Theoretically, we took turns washing, but in reality, it only got done on my days. On his days, we stacked dishes in the sink and they sat until my day rolled around. It wasn't as unfair as it sounds, the way I'm telling it. Apart from faking going to school and faking doing homework, I didn't have a lot to do, whereas my dad was always hustling ways to make money. He had sometimes-work as security at an office building, nights, and then days when he wasn't sleeping, he was delivering newspapers, trimming hedges, whatever he could find to make ends meet. A couple of times he'd sent my mom and me out to collect cans, but after I ran into a kid I knew, they let me stop.

"Do something about this mess," Dad snarled—his version of a cheery *good morning*, I guess.

"Sure, Dad," I said, reaching for Mom's blue-checked apron, despite the fact that I really needed to pee and could have used a cup of coffee myself.

"What's your plan today," he asked, and then, without waiting for an answer, "School still on break? Good. I need you to go around to Clement's and tell 'im I got a dog for 'im to look at, a good one. Mean as hell, be sure you tell 'im that. Tell 'im I'll be home by three — gotta run out to Palmdale on a job, then I'll be back. Three-thirty, latest."

I hated going to Clement's, and if we could just for one day have been like normal people, Dad could have picked up the phone and called Clement himself. But our phone had been cut off for three months — well, two since we lost Dad's cell service too. You'd be surprised how little you really need a phone. It's a little embarrassing, sure, to tell people I'm not allowed to get phone calls at home, but they fall for it. I don't have a lot of close friends — I guess from moving around and skipping school so much.

It was supposed to be my sophomore year, but the thing is, I'd been really tired on the first day of school, so I hadn't gone, and then the second day you were supposed to turn in all this paperwork that obviously I didn't have since they'd given it out the first day, so I hadn't gone to that either. Then there was a three-day weekend, and by the time school started up again, on a Tuesday, I felt like it had already started without me. So I went to the public library and hung around, checked Facebook and Instagram. Nobody had written on my wall or DM'd me. It was like school was saying if I didn't want it, it didn't want me either, no problem. So I checked out some books and went to the park. Later, I told my dad I had a light schedule and that we were allowed to leave at noon if we didn't have classes. He wouldn't have known. I watched the mailbox for a few weeks to be sure nothing came from school, but nothing ever did. Maybe they didn't even notice I was missing, or maybe they figured I'd switched to private school, or moved away. Maybe they thought when my mom died she left us a big insurance policy and we'd used it to relocate to a tropical island.

"Okay, Dad," I said slowly, wishing he'd ask me why I hate going over to Clement's so much, but he didn't, of course. My mother would have known, without me struggling to find a way to say.

"Good." He ran his hands under the tap, dried them on his work pants, and grabbed his keys from the hook by the back door.

"Have a good day, Dad," I told him, getting up on tiptoe to kiss his bristly cheek. I was sixteen, but I barely reached his chin. Mom was small and I guess I will be too. My feet are just starting to fit into the sneakers she used to wear, and I can wear her sweaters, although her pants are a bit short on me.

"Go on," Dad said, brushing me away impatiently. "And take some food down to that dog. I don't want it to be all wore out when Clement gets here. Give it—" He looked around the cluttered kitchen and shrugged. "Give it that leftover macaroni."

The pasta in question was three days old and probably too spicy for a dog. It had certainly not sat well in my stomach, which is why there was still some left despite the meagerness of our cupboard.

"I don't know if a dog can eat that . . ." I began, but Dad was gone.

## *Jared and Jocelyn*

I am not a bad dog, but I did a bad thing.

I had a boy once, and before that, I had a mother, and seven brothers and sisters, although it's difficult to remember them beyond their scents, ripe and musky, smelling of something good and rich, clean fur and milk. My favorite was my littlest sister, the one called Marky by the woman who helped our mother care for us. Marky's eyes opened several days after mine, and sometimes I would help her find a teat, nudging her toward the pink nubs at our mother's belly, so that she could drink before our brothers pushed her aside. That's all I can recall of Marky, besides her good smell. Our mother was creamy white with just a few golden brown speckles, the color of dry kibble, and she smelled delightfully of kibble and milk. She would lick us each in turn, up and down our bodies that seemed to grow fatter each day, beneath our brown or black or cream coats, leaving us clean and damp and ready to squat onto our shredded papers.

I missed my mother when I left her, but my boy was perfect. Jared was six years old, big and strong enough to lift me onto the bed before I was able to jump up, and later, when I finally outweighed him, he could flop over onto my back and ride me, sideways, belly against my back, his arms trailing the floor on one side of me, his feet on the other.

Jocelyn used to tell him, "Jared, don't ride Bear. You're too heavy," but we ignored her, Jared and me. I would carry him through the house, through the clean bright living room and the dark, cool-smelling dining room, across a carpet rich and dense with odors. In the kitchen, we'd stop and I'd get a drink from my special dish, and then we'd lumber down the back steps, Jared's fists tight in my fur, hurting a bit but not enough to make me shake him off. Jared was my burden, my joy, and my purpose, but the others helped me with him too. We were a close pack, small, but in harmony. Every morning before he left for work, Jared's father Michael would give him one soft kiss against the top of his head. Then he would pat my head, too, and say, "Take care of Jared, today, Bear. Good boy. Good dog."

I was a good boy. I was a good dog. But I did a bad thing.

# The Bad Thing

Jared was not allowed to leave the yard, and neither was I, except with a leash on, Jocelyn or Michael or the babysitter, Cruz, at the other end. But boys are a lot like puppies, and sooner or later they will challenge the rules. Jared had sneaked out of the yard a few times before, just to walk on the sidewalk or down to the corner, his hand tight in my ruff, knowing that he was safe with me, that rules or not, I would protect him.

Cruz had caught us once, and had given me a swat on my rear end with a newspaper. She was not allowed to hit Jared, but she knelt before him and held his shoulders in her hands and spoke very sternly to him, and I knew that we were both having the *bad dog* feeling. "*Mijo,*" Cruz said seriously, "you bad boy. No leave yard, Mama say. No leave yard, not safety."

Sometimes when Cruz was not listening, Jared would make fun of her, of her gentle way of speaking, of her humble way of walking, toes pointed in. But we both loved her, and I appreciated the way she helped keep Jared safe. Sometimes she would slip us treats too — cookies or bubble gum for Jared, biscuits she brought from home for me, both forbidden by Jocelyn, who seemed to be our alpha, despite the way she would often lower her voice and dip her head, showing submission to Michael.

On the bad day, Michael had gone to work, and Jocelyn was ready to go, waiting on the porch with her briefcase and her keys, tapping her foot impatiently, waiting for Cruz. I wished I could tell her that Cruz was still far away, too far for me to hear the rumble of the bus arriving at Lincoln Boulevard, three blocks east, too far for me to smell Cruz's good odor of chicken and spice. Jocelyn craned her neck, looking up and down the block, and finally Jared got tired of waiting with her and got up. I stood too, waiting for him to climb aboard, but he took off down the steps, out onto the sidewalk, and down the block, yelling back over his shoulder, "I'll see if she's coming, Mommy!"

Jocelyn shrieked and took off down the steps in her strange small shoes with long spikes for heels, but I was way ahead of her, bounding alongside Jared, making myself a barrier between him and the cars that raced along our street. Even now, I feel my tail go low and tuck between my back legs, remembering with shame, but the truth is, I was glad, in that moment, to be running alongside my boy, protecting him from danger, with his mother loping behind us, all of a pack.

Jared stopped at the corner, and I shoved against him, pushing him a bit farther onto the safety of the cement. But in that instant a small, brown-skinned woman dressed in white pants and a white tunic turned the corner across the street. Jared called out, "Cruz," although of course it wasn't Cruz at all. If he'd only sniffed deeply, or really looked at her, he would have known that, but humans don't look and smell and listen carefully, always. Jared shouted just as Jocelyn called from behind us, first to Jared, and then to me. I am a good dog, and I respond when my name is called.

"Bear! Jared! Come here!" Jocelyn shrieked. "Jared! *Bear!*"

Of course I couldn't go to her; my job was to stay with Jared—but I turned to look back at her, to try to explain with my eyes and my tail, and in that moment, Jared leapt into the street, after Cruz who wasn't Cruz, without waiting for the cars to stop, without waiting for me, or for his mother.

I leapt a second after him, less than that, and I heard the terrible screech of brakes and whine of tires on asphalt, like the cries of a thousand dogs, and then horns blaring, and beneath it all, the awful thick thud of soft flesh colliding with unforgiving metal. Horns, cries, Jocelyn's scream that was more like the heartbroken cry of a suffering dog than anything I'd heard from human throats.

Jared lay half beneath the car, half out from under it, nothing between him and the blue sky, and he looked fine, and he smelled fine, still like

Jared, like peanut butter and boy sweat and cotton. I licked his face and tasted salt, and I smelled blood. It was Jared's blood, spreading out beneath his small body and his perfect unmarked head. I licked him again and nudged him, wanting him to get up, but even as I did, even as Jocelyn dropped down onto the street, her hands frantically pushing at Jared's chest, her mouth lowering to his mouth, the smell of her nearly unbearable with its density of grief, its sharp spice of fear and panic, even then, I knew. I sat down and I put my head back.

I howled.

## CHAPTER THREE

# *Sorry, Kool Lights Company*

The basement is a scary place. The only light comes from a weak yellow bulb that hangs over the stairwell. It's mostly a storage area, with wooden partitions sectioning off little cubbyholes stuffed with suitcases, cardboard boxes, tied-off garbage bags, and boxes marked "Easter Decs" or "Navidad." Most of the junk is abandoned, I guess, but even my dad has never bothered to pull it all out and sort it for a yard sale, it's such obvious trash. I'm sure there are rats in there, and cockroaches, and plenty of spiders.

The dog was tied to the banister. Dad had left him just enough rope to lie down if he scrunched close to the rail. When I came down the stairs, the dog got up, and I froze for a moment. I'm not a dog person, or, truly, an any-animal kind of person. Mostly what we have in my neighborhood are the aforementioned Halloween-type forms of wildlife, plus pigeons, crows, and squirrels, which aren't much more than furry-tailed rats, from what I can see. So I won't say I was scared of dogs, but this one was big, his shoulders rising past my waist when he stood, and his head was as large as mine. He thumped his tail on the stair and gave me kind of a friendly look, but I wasn't buying it. Looks can be deceiving, in case you've never noticed. Pit bulls actually have sort of the prettiest faces of any dogs, with supermodel cheekbones and friendly smiles, and they'll rip your heart out given half a chance. This dog was no pit, but still, I wasn't taking any chances.

"Here," I said, setting a paper plate of pasta on the bottom step and scrambling away fast. The dog sniffed at it, then turned away. I could swear he sighed.

"I'll bring some water when I get back," I told him. "And you better not poop anywhere, or my dad's gonna be pissed." But what choice did he have, really? If he had to go, he had to go.

I fooled around in the kitchen as long as I could, washing the dishes, wringing out the wet rags. I scraped the pasta bowl clean and tied the trash bag, and then I couldn't stall anymore. I had to get over to Clement's to deliver the message, or face my dad with why not when he came back.

Clement's is a dive. One of the parking slots in front is permanently occupied by a broken-down pickup that Clement must have parked there about fifty years ago. There's an ancient pay phone out front, but you wouldn't want to use it if you saw all the gray gummy junk crusted on the receiver and sliming down the metal cord.

Once inside, the thrills continue. First you make your way past this rack of magazines with screaming-loud article titles like "Large Lovely Ladies" and "Big-Busted Beauties," and yeah, they're exactly what you think they are. Clement has apparently never heard of the proverbial plain brown wrapper. After you work your way through a maze of dusty wine bottles and boxes and a single pathetic rack of necessities like toilet paper, ancient baby formula, Kotex, and corn nuts, you're in beer land: six glass-doored coolers displaying every kind of beer known to humanity, plus an entire case just for Colt 45 and Miller Light. And then, lucky you, you get to the counter: rows of gum, breath mints, Life Savers, little packs of aspirin, tiny bottles of mouthwash, cigarette lighters, condoms, and thousands of brands of cigarettes, including the brand that murdered my mom.

Okay, that's not fair. Nobody made her smoke them. Sorry, Kool Lights Company. I'll bet you're a wonderful company full of wonderful people with terrific families. And every one of those families has a mom, and I hope they all die hacking their lungs out into a bloody Kleenex while their kids sit on the stoop wishing for ice cream.

No, I don't.

Well, I sort of do.

If you are a female, aged thirteen or older, you probably know the kind of "I can see your underwear" leer Clement gives every girl or woman who walks through the doors, and if you are a male, please don't ever leer at anyone, because it's revolting.

Clement has mostly normal features, but his eyes are weird. They're like reptile eyes, round, hardly ever blinking. They are a weird pale oceaney color that might be attractive on someone else. Clement's skin is bad—pockmarked from acne or perhaps from some horrible disease that caused him to lose his mind and turn into the leering, drooling Mr. Disgusto who stared at me now, leaning really far over the counter to try to see down my shirt. There's not much there to see, actually, but when I am ready to share, it definitely won't be with Clement.

"Hey, baby," Clement said in his horrible raspy voice, all fake-friendly.

"Hello," I said abruptly. "My dad sent a message for you." I was hoping the mention of my father would scare him off, but Clement grinned even wider and reached his hand toward my face. I stepped back and he laughed. I put my hand in my pocket and fingered the little piece of blue sea glass I keep for luck.

"You got a hair on your mouth," Clement said reasonably. "You want it there, fine with me."

I felt my face growing hot, which is completely unfair because he was the one who should have felt embarrassed. "My dad says come by our house after three o'clock. He has a dog for you."

"Ah, yeah." Clement seemed to lose focus on me for a second. "Big one? Mean fellow?"

Turning to leave, I remembered what my dad had said. "Yeah. Big and bad."

"You want to take a soda, honey?" Clement offered. Cold soda sounded good, but I shook my head.

"Too good to take a soda from Clement, huh?" he said sadly. I couldn't help it. Jerk or not, I couldn't stand anybody accusing me of being stuck-up.

"I'm not too *good* to take a soda, I just don't want one, okay?"

Clement came around from behind the counter and a cold current of fear moved over my skin. I knew I should run out of the store, but I was afraid and embarrassed and ashamed, all mixed up, and I didn't know exactly why.

"Tell you what," Clement said softly, right behind me now. "I bring the sodas to your place a little early. One for you, one for me. We drink them and wait for your daddy together."

Inside my head, I was screaming *don't come early!* But outside, my lips were pressed tight together and I couldn't move. Something touched my shoulder, very lightly. And then the bell jangled and the door came open and I came to life again. I bolted and ran.

The man who had come into the store barely got out of my way as I pushed by him on my way out, and even halfway down the block I could hear his laughter, deep and throaty, and Clement's above it, higher pitched and mean edged, like a knife.

BEAR THREE

## It Was True, What He Said

Cruz came every day, because Michael was afraid to leave Jocelyn alone. Cruz fed me and took me for a walk around the block every morning, then at night before she went home. Afternoons, Jocelyn would sit in the rocking chair in Jared's bedroom, and I would lie in a bar of sun that slanted in through the high window, my head resting on her foot. Cruz would come in and out, bringing the mail or a cup of tea for Jocelyn, answering the phones.

At night, when Cruz unsnapped my leash after our walk, I'd sometimes consider begging to go home with her, but I never did. I thought that my place was with Michael and Jocelyn, though our pup was gone. I had loved Jared with my entire heart, but I also knew that the humans might make more pups for us to tend together.

It went on for a time: eat supper, walk, sleep, eat breakfast, walk, provide what comfort I could to Jocelyn, then sleep again. After many days, one day Cruz didn't come, and after Michael left for work, Jocelyn got back into bed. She wouldn't get up, not to feed me, not to walk me, not even to open the door so that I might go into the yard and do my business there. When Michael came home, I'd shamed myself with a puddle by the front door. He glanced at it, then looked at me with colder eyes than he'd had when Jared was alive. He stalked into the kitchen and stood, alpha male, surveying the mess there: dishes, papers, a dripping faucet. I whined low and slunk close to Michael, tail low, head low, ready to show my throat, apologizing as best I could in a way another dog could not have refused.

"Shut up," Michael said angrily, kicking at me with his hard leather shoe. I lowered myself farther, belly scraping the cold kitchen floor, but instead of forgiving, instead of scratching my ruff or patting my back, he kicked again, hard this time in my ribs, and I shamed myself with a puppy yelp. He kicked again, and then he grabbed something off the kitchen counter—a wooden spoon, I think—and smacked my head with it, smacked my shoulders and my rump and my legs, and kicked me again, and cursed me all the while, angry words flying from his mouth, fury and pain and the rank bitter odor of frustrated male, adult male, angry male human suffusing the air.

"You were supposed to protect him!" Michael yelled. "You were supposed to look after him, you bastard! You should have *died* to protect him!"

I didn't know what I could do to make the beating stop, but I knew exactly what I had done wrong, and if Michael had wanted to get down on his knees and chew at my throat with his poor human teeth, I would have allowed it. It was true, what he said. They had given me their pup to watch over, and I had let a car get him.

My head throbbed and one foreleg screamed with pain—the sharp edge of the wooden spoon had caught it hard, right on the bone, and I could go no lower, sobbing like a puppy, and yet Michael kicked and hit again, and then Jocelyn flew into the kitchen, light and feathery in her nightgown that still smelled of Jared, and of old happiness. She threw herself against her husband's back, caught the wooden spoon in one hand and hammered at his neck with the other, shouting, "No, no, no, Michael, no! Not this! Not in Jared's name!"

And then they were on the floor. He lay face down, and there were tears like Jared's tears, as if Michael were a man no longer, but only a child himself, tears wetting the floor as his shoulders heaved and shook. Jocelyn lay on top of him, smoothing his hair with one hand, covering her face with the other, and after a long time I was able to pull myself to the back door and press against it, hurting everywhere, tasting blood that dripped from my forehead into my mouth, and finally I slept.

# A Gentle Man

"His name is Bear," Jocelyn said tentatively. I could smell doubt and regret rising off her. I could smell her instinct to flee, then, and if she had, I would have run right beside her. Instead she took the pen the man slid across the counter toward her and wrote something on a sheet of paper.

"Hey, Bear," the man said gently, coming around the counter. He knelt and let me smell his brown hand: dog, cat, rabbit, kibble, alfalfa, rat, water, blood, human sweat, lettuce, meat, bleach. I liked the man's easy, soft way of speaking, but his odors were confusing. There was fear layered into the good smells, and lots of cat too.

"He's big, but he's gentle," Jocelyn said. "He likes everyone."

"What happened to his eye?" The man touched the sore place over my eye very gently, and I held back my growl. "His leg bad too."

I still wore a dirty bandage around my front leg, but it didn't hurt much anymore. My muscles were a bit sore, but it was my heart that ached the most. Michael had not been able to forgive me, and Jocelyn was thick and heavy with grief. Something bad was happening to my pack, my pack that had already suffered the worst that can be.

"He—he was beaten," Jocelyn said at last. "His owner beat him. That's why I'm turning him over to you. Please! Will he find a good home—will he go to someone who will love him? He's a very good dog, loyal and smart."

I licked her hand, forgiving her for whatever was happening that was causing her such pain.

"Well," the man said. "First off, if he's not yours legal, you can't give him up."

Neither of them spoke for a long moment.

"He's mine," Jocelyn said finally. "Look, it was my husband who hurt him. But please! He was out of his mind—we lost our son."

And then, horribly, Jocelyn began to cry, big wracking sobs, as the man and I looked at each other, helpless, both of us.

Jocelyn pushed the paper across the counter. "I'm sorry, Bear," she said hoarsely. And then she was gone.

The man knelt again and snapped a plastic leash around my neck. "You hungry, boy?" he asked. He tugged on the leash and I followed him into a cold, damp-smelling room full of smaller rooms, each barred across the front. Dogs were everywhere and the smell, the sound, was overwhelming. I cringed against the man's leg and he laughed.

"Now, come on," he said. "You too big to be slinkin' roun' like a puppy. Come on here and I'll fix you a dish."

He half pushed, half led me into one of the enclosures, set down a metal dish of water, and shut the door. There was nowhere to lie that wasn't wet, but after a few minutes the man came back with another metal dish, this one full of dry food, and a folded towel. He shook the towel out, and I was able to fit most of myself onto it. The food didn't smell bad, but I wasn't hungry. I stretched my paws out before me, let my head drop down onto them, and tried to believe that Jocelyn might really be coming back.

## CHAPTER FOUR

# A Nice Little Lady

The new kid was nice-looking, actually—dark hair, dark eyes, skin the color of brown leaves. He wore loose Hawaiian print board shorts, even though it was January, and a big black hoodie, open at the throat. He was lounging on the stoop in front of our building, deep in a book, and when he could no longer ignore me standing there, he glanced up and went immediately back to his book while grunting, "Hey."

I'd thought he was around my age, but when he looked up at me he seemed older, with deep brackets on either side of his mouth and purple shadows beneath his eyes.

"I'm Candace," I told him. "Everybody calls me Candy, but I don't really like it." He ignored me, turning a page of his paperback.

"'Cause I'm not that sweet," I said at last, getting annoyed. "But I gotta say, my manners are a whole lot better than yours."

The boy's mouth twitched then. "Right," he said, closing his book. "Maybe they oughta call you Lemon."

He stood up, lazily unfolding his long legs, and pushed a clump of brown hair out of his eyes. When he set his book on the stoop, I saw that it was a college text: *Fundamentals of Organic Chemistry*. So he was at least eighteen or nineteen.

"Very funny," I said. "Ha, ha."

He grinned and stuck out a hand, which I ignored. "*Mucho gusto*, Lemon," he told me. "I'm Carlos. You can call me Carl if it's too hard to pronounce. I answer to either one."

I felt my face get hot. What kind of idiot couldn't pronounce *Carlos*? "So—how come you're always sitting out here?" I asked.

"Hmm," he said. "Well, I like to read. And there are seven little reasons I can't read in the apartment." He began to tick them off on his fingers. "Marta, Ana, Vittoria, Miguel, Oscar, Sam . . ."

I had to laugh. "You're lucky," I told him. "My place gets lonely, since my dad's hardly ever around." Then I blushed. Had I just met a semi-cute guy and within the first five minutes told him I was lonely, that my dad was never home, and practically invited him up?

Carlos didn't pick up on it, though, or perhaps he was a gentleman. I liked that he didn't ask about my mom, and in return I didn't ask about his.

"Are Rafael and Luisa your aunt and uncle?" I asked, and he nodded. "How come you never help them out?" I said, and I felt my face get hot again. I was being nosy. But Carlos didn't seem to mind. He just shrugged.

"I do, with money," he said. "I work nights, and I give most of my pay to Tía Luisa. I only keep a little for bus fare and . . . stuff. You know." He grinned. "If I want to buy a girl a Coke or something."

At this rate, I thought I might as well just stay red and claim I had a permanent sunburn. The way Carlos was grinning at me, he must have thought he was pretty clever, or that I was pretty desperate. I frowned to show him I wasn't having any and started to turn away.

"Where you going, Lemon? I didn't mean to scare you away."

"Believe me, your chances of scaring me are smaller than microscopic," I told him. "I've got to go feed my dad's dog."

Carlos eyed the dish in my hands. "Oh, yeah. That dog in the basement? What you gonna do with him? He's been down there two days already."

"Don't worry, we're getting rid of him. My dad sold him to—you know that guy that runs the liquor store? Clement?"

Carlos's face darkened. "Yeah, I know him. I know him enough that I don't let Marta and Ana go in there no more." He looked me up and down and then shook his head. "And you shouldn't be goin' in there either."

I made a dismissive sound with my lips, a little "phffff," as though what he'd said were ridiculous, though in fact I agreed with him wholeheartedly.

"I don't need anybody to tell me what to do or where to go," I said firmly. "I look after myself."

Carlos nodded. "Cool. Just be careful, dude. I'm serious. Clement's a freak."

I started down the steps to the basement, not entirely disappointed when Carlos made as if to follow. He slipped ahead of me and got the door open, then switched on the naked bulb.

"You shouldn't leave that dog alone in the dark like that," he said. "That's not cool. And look, you didn't even give him a blanket or nothing."

It was true. The dog looked pathetic, all hunched up next to the banister rail, blinking against the light. I flushed. "He's not my responsibility," I said huffily. "He belongs to Clement. I'm just feeding him so he doesn't drop dead before they come to get him."

The dog didn't look in danger of death, just very uncomfortable. His coat was dirty and matted, and I was ashamed to notice two or three heaps of droppings where he'd had no choice but to go. He was standing in wetness, too, and the basement had begun to reek of a combination of dog doo, dog pee, and just plain old dog.

"Okay, boy," Carlos said, easing his hand toward the dog's collar. "Let me get that rope off you, and we'll get you something to eat." He turned to me. "You bring him any water? Go upstairs and get some, and I'll get that rope off him."

I obeyed, thinking I ought to protest his bossy tone but secretly glad he was taking over. I didn't really care much about the dog one way or another, but it seemed a shame to make him suffer needlessly. Having to belong to Clement would be suffering enough. Trudging up the steps, I thought about it. Clement probably wanted the dog to guard the store at night. It'd be lonely, I supposed, but warm enough, and daytimes there'd be people in and out all the time.

The only thing was, my dad had sold Clement another dog not a month or so earlier. I hadn't thought about that one in a while—a big red pit with a torn ear and a distinctly nasty disposition. My dad hadn't asked me to watch that one—he'd taken it right over to Clement and had come back with a fistful of fives and tens and a cold Colt 45 in a paper bag to celebrate his good fortune high style.

No doubt that dog had run away. Clement was probably mean to it. Or maybe it had been too much for him to handle—I hadn't even liked looking at it, a big muscular dog with teeth the length of the last joint of my finger. At any rate, I'd never seen it around the store or heard it barking.

When I got back with the water, Carlos hadn't gotten the dog off the rope. He was sitting, holding his hand for the dog to smell, and the dog was sniffing politely enough, but growling, way back in his throat, almost to softly to hear.

"It's okay, boy," Carlos said. "It's okay. I'm not gonna hurt you, man." The dog made some kind of a decision because his growling shifted to a soft, high-pitched whine that seemed almost ridiculous coming from his massive frame. "Okay," Carlos said. "Okay." He reached past the dog and worked at the knotted rope, finally unfastening it. The dog moaned, stood up, stretched, and shook all over, hard. "Okay, give him the water," Carlos said. I set it before the big dog, who lapped at it so thirstily that I felt ashamed. "Why don't you get a bag and a dustpan and pick up some of the crap," he suggested.

I bristled. "Why don't you?"

"He's not my dog," he protested.

I shrugged. "Mine neither."

But I was going for the trash can when the basement door flew open. A burst of hoarse, too-hearty laughter, and an answering laugh, high pitched and shrill. Fifteen seconds in duration but packed with all the information I needed to know. My dad, drunk. And with him, Clement.

Carlos had worked his hand into the ruff around the Aussie's neck, but now the dog pulled away and backed against the stairs, whining again. My dad sized it all up—me, the boy, the dog—and I saw him consider and discard an array of reactions (anger, shame, suspicion), then settle on contempt.

"What you doin', girl? Down here makin' a pet out of a wild dog?"

Carlos looked up at my father, eyes narrowed.

Clement took his opportunity to leer, shielded as he was from my father's gaze. "I hope that's all she's been doin' down here with my buddy Carl," he said nastily. My father's back stiffened. Drunk or not, I was his daughter and he wasn't going to let anyone besmirch my honor, unless maybe he chose to take that privilege for himself.

"What you talking about?" he demanded, whirling on Clement. "You got something you wanna say? Say it out like a man."

The alcohol slurred his words, and I knew his reaction was more about the drink than about me, but in those days, I'd take what protection I could get. Maybe they'd fight, and my dad could kick Clement's ass once and for all. I'd tell him about all the inappropriate comments Clement had made, the looks, the nasty touch on my shoulder . . .

But Clement was grinning sheepishly, palms up. "I didn't mean nothing, man. That's a nice girl you've got there. I know you're proud of her, man. Looks like her mom too. Nice little lady like her mom was."

My father blinked hard, and glanced from me to Carlos to the dog and back to Clement. "Gimme the money," he said abruptly.

Clement took a sheaf of bills from his front pocket but didn't hand it over. "Got to check out the merchandise first."

"Deal's a deal, man," my dad protested, but Clement was already standing over the dog, gazing down at it appraisingly. "Big bastard," he said softly. "Nice."

He sounded so gentle that I almost thought he might feel some affection for the dog. Was it possible that even scum like Clement could have a weakness, a secret goodness, that made him vulnerable and less of a monster?

But even as I thought it, Clement drew his foot back. I saw Carlos's face tighten and his hand, the one that wasn't buried in the dog's ruff, came out, as if to shield the dog or stop Clement, but he wasn't fast enough. Clement landed a hard, powerful kick in the dog's midsection, and in that instant the sounds were all combined—the blow against the dog's solid body, Carlos's furious cry, the dog's scream, melding into a snarl and a snap of teeth, and then Carlos's grunt of pain.

The dog collapsed in a heap, shaking and growling and crying all at once, and Carlos leapt up, holding his hand as it streamed blood down his wrist and into his sleeve.

"Oh, you gotta be tougher than that, little man," I heard Clement say, and it wasn't clear who he was talking to, Carlos or the dog, but it didn't matter. As I slammed out of the basement and tore up the steps, sobbing, I heard my father's booming laughter and, oddly, amid it all, I felt a swift sudden stab of anger at my mother. *You ought to be here*, was what I thought. *You ought to be here with me.*

# Blue-Haired Death

Most days at the shelter were good. I learned, though, to beware when all of the little rooms and cages were full; that was when the blue-haired girl would choose a dog to die. She walked past our cages slowly, consulting her clipboard and nodding and making pencil notes. She spoke softly to us, and some dogs would move toward the bars and put their noses against her hand, smelling her, licking her, asking her to love us, or at least to let us live. Those who were most afraid would push against the back wall, sometimes shaking, and if I could not see the trembling flanks of the others, I could smell their hope and their shit and piss and fear. It was the ones who were most afraid who were usually chosen. Was it cruelty? Because she didn't seem cruel, the Death Girl. She seemed sad. I could smell it on her. When she scratched my head through the wire, I thought I sensed regret.

The little dogs had a better chance than the big ones; one day I realized that every big dog that had been at the shelter when I arrived was gone—a few taken by strangers, most chosen by the blue-haired Death Girl. But many little dogs remained, bouncing inside their small enclosures, whining, barking like puppies though many were clearly older than I.

Sometimes the Gentle Man took me out, snapping a plastic leash around my neck, and ran with me around the block once or twice, jogging along beside me and sucking on a cigarette at the same time. He'd pick up my droppings with a plastic bag, though what he wanted them for I can't imagine. Once when the Death Girl lingered before my enclosure, whispering to herself and, I think, maybe crying, he came to her and put his arm around her and said, "Not this big boy, Rachel. I gotta feelin' about him. Somebody gonna pick him soon."

And then she'd nodded, looking up at him, smiling through her tears, and she'd moved on to an overweight pit mix who had an ugly cough and rheumy, red-rimmed eyes.

And somebody did pick me, soon enough, for that was what this place was—a home for dogs that had lost their packs. Why the killing, I don't know, but many times I would hear people come in bright and excited, laughing, watch them move between the enclosures, picking, comparing, and watch them go out again with a dog on a plastic leash, smelly and matted but radiating hope and pleasure. I never wanted that. I wanted Jocelyn, and Cruz, and most of all, Jared. I even wanted Michael. I didn't want strangers. I didn't care, really, if the Death Girl picked me, and led me to the Bad Room on a plastic leash, and left me there, dead, for the Gentle Man to carry out to the dumpster. But then, one day, I did care.

He was a boy older than Jared but not quite grown, and he had short hair where Jared's had been long, and he smelled of grape candy, which Jared had not liked. But he reminded me of Jared, the way he bounced up on his toes when he walked. The way he pressed his hand flat against the bars of my enclosure and waited, without calling me, without speaking.

I went to him and sniffed. I pressed my cheek against his hand, not minding the coldness of the wire, just smelling him and wanting to be his. Then he called to someone and a man came over and said in a worried voice, "This is a big one, Alfie."

Alfie grinned, working my fur between his fingers. "I like him. Lookit his tail. He's like a German shepherd, but he's fluffier, like an Aussie. And lookit his shoulders—he's strong."

And then the Gentle Man came over and opened my door and I stepped out and pressed myself to Alfie's leg and he knelt and put his arms around my shoulders and said, "Good boy. Good dog."

Those words fell down around me like sweet rain. I licked Alfie's hand and tried hard to push Jared out of my mind.

CHAPTER FIVE

## *Candy and the Deep Blue Sea*

The waves crashed against the shore again and again, creeping a little farther out each time, until there was a broad stretch of dark sand between me and the edge of the ocean; the bottom of the sea, naked in a way it is not meant to be seen, smooth and exposed, dotted with broken shells and sea glass. Seagulls and a single sandpiper darted around the rocks each time a wave went out, snapping up tiny sand crabs left exposed by the receding foam.

I loved the rush of water to the shore, the wildness of it, and the steadiness. Looking out at the chunky green water, and beyond it, the sparkling blue expanse that melts into the paler blue of the sky, I felt very small. Nothing that I could do would matter; no mistake I might make, no word I could say or leave unsaid would make any difference at all.

If I disappeared, the water would still rush to the shore. Pelicans would still cruise in V formation overhead, the leader of the V dropping gracefully back as another moved forward in perfect synchrony to take his place. If I waded into that deep water and let the waves carry me out too far to ever swim back again, if I slipped beneath the foaming surface, the water would still rush toward the shore, then pull away again. The cold winter sun would still glint against the sand, turning it into a cold field of diamonds.

# *Alfie*

Alfie's room smelled good: like worn socks and human laundry, rich with odors of sweat and food and grass and soil. When we first got there, Alfie sat on his bed doing homework on a clipboard, and I lay on the carpet beside him, enjoying the warmth and the peace and the human noises, instead of the incessant barking of dogs.

That first night, Alfie's mother told me to sleep on a pile of towels she'd stacked in the kitchen, and it was perfectly comfortable, much nicer than the shelter had been, of course, though I was lonely and wished I could sleep with Alfie. But in the middle of the night, after the mother and father had gone to bed, Alfie crept out of his room and down the hall, his feet making a pleasant scritchety sound on the carpet. When he got to the kitchen, he stood and looked at me for a long time, and then he went to the fridge and tore off a chunk of chicken meat from the carcass the family had shared for dinner. I couldn't believe it when he held it out to me—it was greasy and salty and delicious, and I gobbled it and licked his fingers clean. Then he knelt and put his arms around my neck and huddled close to me. His arm pressed against my injured front leg and it hurt, because he was bony without much padding, and beneath my thick coat, I was too. But nothing could have made me move a single inch. It felt so good, to have a piece of chicken in my belly and a warm boy cuddled next to me to watch over through the night.

CHAPTER SIX

## *Not Exactly a Dream Date*

"How's your hand?"

Carlos looked up reluctantly from his book, appearing distracted, then met my eyes and seemed to recognize me, suddenly. He held his hand up to show me the clean white bandage around his forefinger.

"Stupid dog," I said, trying to commiserate. "You should've known better than to step into a dogfight."

"It wasn't a fight," Carlos said mildly. "It was one guy kicking a defenseless animal." He winced and tucked his injured hand beneath his arm. "Well. Maybe not so defenseless." His long legs dangled over the edge of the cement stoop.

I laughed. "Uh, yeah. I'd say."

Carlos seemed completely immune to the yellow sleeveless tank top I'd put on mostly, if we're being honest, because I realized I'd be walking right by him on my way to the bus stop, and also in celebration of the bright cloudless sky, and not a drop of rain forecast. In fact, he'd already dipped back into his book, a hank of glossy dark hair falling over his forehead in a way that was somehow quite appealing.

"Um, so, I guess I'll see you around," I said lamely, embarrassed to still be standing there, but feeling just as awkward about turning and walking away.

"Yeah, hold on. I'm almost done," Carlos said brusquely. He looked around and picked up a dry leaf off the stoop to use as a bookmark. "Where you headed?"

I shrugged. "The pool, I think. Gotta do something to celebrate the last day of break, right?"

He met my eyes with a steady gaze. "Break?"

31

I felt my face get hot. "You know . . . winter break? Christmas?"

Carlos nodded. "For those of us who go to school," he said. "But you, Lemon? I've seen you getting off the bus at the library sometimes, in the middle of the day. I've seen you at the park on my way to work in the afternoons. I don't think you ever go to school." He must have seen something in my face because he cleared his throat. "Not my business," he said gently. "Your secret is safe with me."

I stared at Carlos without answering, refusing to either confirm or deny. "Hang on while I get a towel and I'll go with," he said. He darted into the open doorway just beside the basement steps, and I was left standing there, wondering if I had somehow managed to arrange what could actually be counted as my very first date.

It didn't seem very romantic five minutes later, though, when Carlos came back out with a ragged gray towel and a pair of plaid trunks, a paper sack full of God knew what, and two little girls, the bigger one hanging onto the hem of his sweatshirt, the other hanging onto her sister's wrist, both of them giggling, chattering in Spanish, and looking scared and happy and confused all at the same time. Each girl wore a tiny pink plastic backpack and matching pink plastic sandals I recognized with a sharp pang as being from last summer's stock at the 99. The girls had matching black braids, one with pink clips, the other lavender.

"If you think I'm babysitting—" I began.

Carlos's gaze met mine, and for once he seemed to have lost his confidence. His charcoal eyes seemed to plead with me, and I felt my resolve giving way. "My aunt packed us some stuff," he said sheepishly, holding out the paper sack.

I peeked in: iced white cookies, four or five oranges, a bunch of juice pouches, and a couple of fat foil-wrapped torpedoes that I figured were sandwiches.

"We've got the best cookies, Candy," the bigger girl said happily, letting go of Carlos's belt and grabbing my free hand. I was surprised that she knew my name. I certainly didn't know hers. Her tiny hand was hot and moist and it wiggled in mine like a little animal. "Thank you for taking us swimming, Candy," she said gravely. She poked her sister's foot with one pink sandal, and the littler girl echoed, "Thank you, Candy."

Carlos and I looked at each other. He shrugged and took the brown paper sack and my swim bag in his arms, shoving his own stuff into my bag in a way that seemed a bit presumptuous. I shrugged back, and we headed for the bus stop: not a boy and girl on a date, after all. Still, we had snacks, towels, and bus fare. Life can get worse.

CHAPTER SEVEN

## A Summer's Day in Winter

The pool was what pools are on a bright warm day when you're coming off a week of rain: at first, because we were almost the first to arrive, a shimmering sheer sheet of impossibly inviting clear turquoise blue, and then, within minutes, a seething mass of kids of every size, shape, and color, splashing, screaming, spinning, jumping . . . doing everything, almost, but swimming, because a) most of them probably didn't know how, and b) there wasn't any room.

I'm okay with that—when I want to get laps in, I hit the pool at the adults-only times. It's a world you don't see much in L.A.—people silent, concentrating, and incredibly polite. There's this whole system you have to follow—if you want to get in a lane, and somebody's already there, you stand at the edge and wait till they surface. Then you kind of do this eye-catch, subtle-nod thing that says, *I know you're there, and you know I'm here, so let's agree not to smash into each other.* And it works.

I am not a fast swimmer, or even a very strong one, because I don't actually know most of the strokes. I just get in and start dipping with my arms and kicking, all the while trying not to splash too much. I never learned butterfly, breast, that stuff, because I taught myself. Sometimes I study the other swimmers and try to do what they do.

But there was none of that lap swimming now. I took the girls into the bathroom to shower off, and when we came out Carlos was in the water, waving at us. It was just him, for a moment, a glossy black head of hair and a brown face split by a blinding white grin. I felt my stomach lurch in a weird way and looked away from him.

Then the girls were running to the water, standing at the edge and bouncing in their pink and lavender suits, and Carlos was beckoning to them to jump in. He stood up to show them it was only three or four feet deep, and when he did, I saw that his chest was lean but muscled, delineated by a sparse but definite line of hair that bisected his ribs and headed into the—never mind.

"Ana, jump!" the littler girl shrieked, and her sister looked around, taking a huge breath that puffed out her cheeks and made her look like a brown blowfish. Then she jumped in, shrieking so that she certainly couldn't be holding her breath any longer, and Carlos caught her and threw her up in the air, then set her down in the water, gently, making sure she could stand up. She stood there, chin deep, clutching his shoulder and grinning, overcome with pride.

A gigantic group of chubby blond kids ran along the side of the pool to the deep end as the guard blew his whistle frantically, signaling *walk, don't run*. Carlos was calling, "Vittoria, jump!" and Ana was bouncing up and down in the water, able now to let go of Carlos's shoulder, which was marked with four tiny red crescents where she'd gripped too tightly.

I walked over to Vittoria, a little shy in my one-piece but glad for all those long walks I'd taken in the winter and all the pans of brownies I could have baked but had resisted. I took Vittoria's hand.

"Come on, kid," I told her. "Let's jump in together."

CHAPTER EIGHT

# *They Say Suffering Makes You Noble*

I guess I sort of thought things might go somewhere after that morning at the pool, but Carlos seemed to be either really busy, or just not digging the sight of my chicken legs in the blue suit. I didn't see him for a few days, although I'll admit I was finding reasons to walk outside when I thought he might be there. Whatever. I had enough to do, with my best babysitting customers, twins Dylan and Justin, heading back to third grade. Their mom, Julia, was a teacher who walked them to school every morning, but it was my job to escort the twins home afternoons and stay with them till one of the parents returned. The first time I stopped by the elementary school to pick them up after break ended, I'd walked into the aftercare room and been nearly mowed down, not by the twins, who liked me well enough but were usually focused on Legos and had to be dragged out, but by Vittoria and Ana and a couple more kids who also seemed to be extremely happy to see me, although I wasn't sure exactly who they were. With Vittoria climbing me like a tree and the others pushing me around, hugging and squealing, I must have looked more appealing than usual to the twins, because Dylan got up and came over and took my hand in a somewhat proprietary way, telling the tiny boy who was glued to my thigh, "This is *my* babysitter, me and my brother's."

"Take us, too, Candy," Ana begged, but of course I couldn't. Even if I'd had permission to check the Gomez kids out of school, I wasn't going home.

"Sorry, kiddo," I said, tousling her hair and setting Vittoria carefully on the scuffed floor. "Another time."

I meant it casually, not really planning for it to happen anytime soon — doing that grown-up thing I hate, come to think of it. But when I got home, just as dusk was turning the sky that deep, gorgeous orange you've got to love even though you know it's mostly caused by air pollution, Carlos was sitting on the stoop, book closed for once. "Hey," he said, grinning. His teeth were gorgeously white against his golden skin.

"Hey, back," I said, suddenly shy.

Carlos shoved over so there was room for me to sit. Instead, I leaned against the broken doorbell panel, looking down at him in the deepening twilight.

"Actually, I'm not sitting here waiting for you because I want to see you," Carlos began.

"I didn't think—" I interrupted.

"I mean—" he blurted, and then we stared at each other for a moment before we both cracked up laughing. "What I mean is," he said at last, "I *am* waiting for you, and I *do* want to see you, but I also I got told to wait for you by Tía Luisa."

"Okay," I said, a little confused.

"She says you offered to pick the kids up from school tomorrow," Carlos said. "And she wants to know if you really can do it, because she's got to take Anthony to the doctor."

"I didn't . . ." I protested. "I mean, I sort of did offer, but I didn't say tomorrow . . ."

Carlos frowned. "No worries. I'll just tell her you're busy. Any other day, I could do it, but I'm on split shift for the next two weeks, and I don't get off until nine."

"Well, I probably could do it," I relented, "if she calls and tells them to put me on the pickup list. I don't have to get my regular kids tomorrow."

"My aunt's paying, you know, " Carlos said hastily. "It's not a favor. I mean, it *is*, but it's not *just* a favor." He grinned again and I felt a strange little pull in my tummy.

So that's how I started to feel like Julie Andrews in that movie about the singing nanny with twelve obnoxious kids. Some days I had Gomez kids, some days I had Dylan and Justin, and some days I had all of them, me and the twins walking the Gomez crew home before backtracking to their place. And that's how I started making enough money to stand up to my dad the next time he tried to send me over to Clement's to buy smokes. I had pocket money and even a little grocery money, at least for the essentials: mac and cheese, milk, toilet paper, Tampax, and the occasional package of the world's best food, dried mango slices.

I had just come from the twins' house, and I was tired. Justin was coming down with a cold, and Dylan was just getting over one, and they'd spent the afternoon trying to drive me crazy, Dylan bored and cranky with a rope of snot hanging out of his nose, no matter how many times I wiped it, and Justin exhausted, wanting to keep up with his twin but without the energy to do much more than lie on the couch, prepped to cry. I had twenty bucks in my pocket, though, and another ten promised for the next day, and that felt good, and when my dad flipped open his wallet and folded a fiver, I shook my head.

"Go yourself," I told him. "I'm not buying your cigarettes anymore. They're killing you."

My dad shook his head like there were flies buzzing around it, confusing him. "What? Get up off your ass, girl, and run to Clement's. I need smokes."

"No," I said stubbornly. "Clement's a pervert and I'm not going there anymore. Besides, I went to school today, and then I worked. What did you do?"

The school part was a lie, and the rest wasn't really fair, because at times my dad worked pretty hard, even if he didn't make much. But I could tell from the way he was collapsed in his chair with empty beer cans at his feet and an overflowing ashtray that he'd been home most of the day.

"Ain't that a bitch," he muttered to himself. He stirred as if he would get up off the chair, but maybe it was too much effort. After a minute he picked up his ashtray and started rooting around in it for a butt with some tobacco left in it.

I went into my room, careful not to slam the door. I felt proud and ashamed at the same time. My dad had always been a drunk, and he'd always been kind of rough and sometimes a little mean. But there had been good times too. Maybe my mom had smoothed his rough edges and reminded him of how a family man should act. Now he just never seemed to care. I looked out my window, but the stoop was bare beneath the heavy yellow moon.

I have to admit, I never gave even one thought to that miserable dog we'd had chained in the basement, then passed to Clement. But maybe I should have. They say suffering makes you noble and sensitive and all that crap. The truth is, suffering makes you selfish. I was suffering that early spring. I missed my mom, and I guess I kind of missed my dad too. I was sad a lot, even when I was flirting with Carlos (yeah, I said it) or joking around with the Gomez kids or mixing oatmeal cookies with the twins. I was sad, and I was selfish, and I was suffering. But probably not as much as that poor dog.

BEAR SEVEN

## *I Thought We Might Be Friends*

I never stopped missing Jared or the rest of my first pack. Sometimes when I lay on my rug in the sunny front hall—I was not allowed on the furniture in this clean new house—I would doze off and awaken confused, listening for the sound of Cruz working upstairs, for Jocelyn's key in the door. It would seem then, for a sleepy moment, that Jared would come bursting through the front door, yelling my name, ready to play fetch or tug-of-war, or that Jocelyn would come in, cold after her long walk from the bus stop, ready to sit down and bury her toes in my warm fur. Then Linda, Alfie's mom, would touch me absently with her foot as she walked to the kitchen, or Alfie would stop and kneel to scratch all around my ears where the fur is so thick it's difficult to penetrate with my hind paw, and I would remember my new home and my new life, grateful for one pack but still longing for the other.

I slept there on the rug, summer and winter, though sometimes Alfie would call me to come into his room and snuggle at night. When that happened, I tried to get back into the hall before morning, because it annoyed Linda to find me anywhere but on my rug in the hall. Sometimes she would vacuum my fur up from the living room where it gathered in loose dust balls, and she would narrow her eyes as if appraising me, as if she were angry or annoyed. But Linda never struck me; no one did, and I was often petted and fussed over by Alfie and his friends, though less so as he grew older and spent more time away from home.

The worst thing that could happen was losing Jared, and that had happened, so there was not much more to fear. Yet one summer the house was full of sorrow, heavy in the voices of my young master, now nearly a man,

40

and his parents, heavy in their scents and in the droop of their shoulders. No one wanted to walk me; Alfie would sometimes take me out late at night, but I'd have to tug to remind him to let me stop at a tree or a hydrant as he spoke into the black box he held in his hand and was seldom without. The sorrow came mostly from Alfie's mother, Linda, though the house was filled with big boys, nearly men, like Alfie, and girls who fixed snacks and carried them to the boys on the patio, giggling and chattering and sometimes stopping to stroke my fur or absently pat the top of my head.

Sometimes Alfie seemed excited, but his mother was nearly always sad, even as she spoke in a bright, artificial voice and carried in cardboard boxes and duffel bags and plastic bags full of new-smelling pillows and towels and sheets.

And the day came when Alfie and his father, Harold, carried it all outside again, and loaded bags and suitcases and boxes into Alfie's beat-up two-seater car, and he hugged his mother and shook hands with his father and just when I thought he'd forgotten all about me, he turned and knelt and put his arm around my neck and kissed the top of my head, fast. Then Alfie jumped in the car and waved and drove away, and Linda sagged against her husband as if something had struck her.

"It's only college, Linny," he said gently, but his words caused her to fold into his chest, sobbing.

"He'll be back," Harold tried again, but Linda wouldn't be comforted.

"He'll be back," she agreed grimly, "but it will never be the same again."

And of course she was right.

I thought Linda and I might become friends, then, in the lonely days after Alfie went away. Harold went out to work, but she didn't, so she had lots of time at home to clean and that's what she did, now more than ever, spending hours on her knees scrubbing floors that seemed clean already, dumping the contents of drawers into paper bags to be carried to the trash, dusting, wiping, and polishing every surface in that clean cold house.

A couple of times Linda gave me the end of her sandwich after she'd finished, absently stroking my head as I ate, and that's what made me think she might be coming to love me, but more often she gave me a cold, narrow-eyed look as if my shedding fur were anything I could help, as if I dirtied her floors and carpets through my own volition. She was lonely and I was lonely, but there seemed no way to bridge the gap; if I went to lie beside her when she took a rare break to lie on the sofa and watch TV, she shooed me away, sending me back to the hall to lie on my rug. When I tried to follow her out the front door for a walk, thinking a companion would comfort her and keep her safer, she spoke sharply to me, telling me to use the dog flap cut into the back door if I needed to relieve myself.

Late one afternoon I was home alone; Linda had gone out in her car, and Harold was at work. The house was cold and empty, and I made my rounds restlessly, sniffing at Alfie's closed door and whining a little, I'll confess, before checking the bedrooms and the downstairs areas: kitchen, dining room, bathroom, living room. I was on my way back to the hall to lie down on my rug when I heard a noise from the kitchen, which had been as empty and silent as expected just a moment before but for the distant sounds of traffic and an occasional squeak of a squirrel outside.

Someone was pushing the window open! I barked a warning.

He was halfway in and halfway out, one long leg thrown over the sill and his torso and head already in our kitchen, a stranger, a bad man, reeking of fear and anger and secrecy and aggression; a stranger who meant us harm. I barked again and flew at him, sinking my teeth into his muscular leg through the thick fabric of his denim pants. Fool that he was, he cursed and kicked at me instead of trying to get away, and I let go long enough to get a firmer grip on him, tugging hard to pull him all the way into the kitchen so I could really get at him, punish him for trying to enter our home without permission, and teach him to keep away.

The bad man must have realized I meant business because now he kicked hard at me and I felt myself fly up in the air, still with my teeth in his pants and his leg, and as my body hit the kitchen table, a stack of magazines fell over, and a vase with flowers, but no real damage was done, either to me or to the kitchen. The stranger cursed and called me the same evil words I remembered from that awful night when Michael had beaten me, but now the words sounded good, tinged as they were with the stranger's pain and fear. I let him go, just long enough for him to get himself out the window again, and then I circled the kitchen, barking threats and warnings, barking of my pride and triumph.

Finally I calmed down a bit, but I stayed in the kitchen, stretched out near the window, ready to keep an eye on it until one of the humans came home to close and lock it again. By the time Linda arrived it was growing dark. I stretched and got up, a bit stiff from the fight, as I heard her car down the street. I'll admit I was proud of myself for the job I'd done. I was eager to share the story with my humans as best I could.

Linda bustled through the back door with her arms full of packages, barely stopping to bump the door shut with her hip before she saw me beneath the open window.

"Why are you in here?" Linda demanded angrily. Her eyes fell on the open window, on the broken vase and the puddle of water and the magazines scattered on the floor. "What have you done?" she demanded again. "Bad dog! Bad, bad boy! Damn it, what did you do?"

I whined, nosing at the floor around the open window. The bad man's smell was strong and rank though he'd been gone for hours. But Linda didn't seem to notice. She knelt to pick up the magazines, then stood and slammed the window shut without noticing the stranger's scent, without seeing the drop of blood on the sill, without realizing my hind leg was stiff and sore where the man had kicked me into the table.

"Get out, you bad dog!" Linda shrieked, holding the back door open. "Now!"

As I slunk past her, she swatted at me with a folded magazine.

# *Country Living*

"I don't know what she's going to tell Alfie," Linda's husband said in a worried voice, reaching over to scratch beneath my collar. "Sorry, boy. But you'll be better off anyway. Not much fun for a big dog like you in a house with no kids, I guess."

I whined softly, sensing guilt and regret in Harold's unaccustomedly tender voice. "But you really shouldn't have gone wild in the kitchen like that," he continued. "That just sent her right over the edge. I think we would've been okay, if not for that little incident."

I blinked, indifferent. I had tried to tell them about the bad man, of course, but it didn't really make a difference to me whether they understood. A dog protects his pack because that's the nature of a dog, not because he wants recognition and praise. In the days since the break-in, I'd tried to stay close to Linda to be sure she was safe, especially during the day when Harold was gone, but she'd banished me to the backyard, tossing my rug outside so I'd have a place to sleep, not seeming to notice that the rug grew damp with dew that first day and never really dried out enough to be comfortable. It didn't matter a lot; my fur is thick and warm, and I could guard the house as easily from outside as from within. It was loneliness that troubled me most, but there'd been little companionship inside since Alfie had left anyway.

Rain drummed steadily on the roof and hood as Harold guided the car through the nearly empty streets. A thought occurred to me—could he be taking me to wherever Alfie had gone, to live with him? I'd have loved to be with my boy again, and with his rowdy, clumsy friends. But there was no smell of Alfie in the streets we traveled. The city smells of humans and cars and traffic on wet asphalt were fading away, replaced by the fresh odor of vegetation, and strange animal scents that were new to me, both frightening and enticing. We passed huge stands of trees, and then mile upon mile of flat, planted fields that smelled of chemicals and of growing things. Finally Harold pulled the car onto a dirt road and turned off the motor. There were trees all around us, dark and foreboding. Instead of getting out right away, he sat and stroked my neck and back, something he'd rarely, or maybe never, done.

"I am sorry, boy," he said softly. "But it's better for you and better for her. You'll find a place, a nice dog like you. Some farmer will want you, or you can live off rabbits and chipmunks, like a wolf. That's what I'd want, if I was a big dog like you."

He pushed opened the car door and scents flooded my muzzle, making me feel dizzy and uncertain. The rain had stopped, at least temporarily, but the air and ground were thick with it; water everywhere, and the smells of animals and soil. Everything about this place was strange. I didn't want to be here. I wanted to go home. I remembered Alfie and Harold coming to choose me, to take me home, and that first night with Alfie, the warm chicken in my belly, the warm boy snuggled against me.

Harold unsnapped my leash. I shivered and sunk low to the floor, but he pushed me out of the car, and as I got up to stand shakily on the muddy road, overwhelmed by sounds and smells, he slammed the door shut and backed the car out fast. I barked and chased the car, wary of the wheels but terrified that he would abandon me here, so far from our home.

And that is what he did.

I knew what a chipmunk was; we'd had them in the bushes at the edge of the yard at Jocelyn and Michael's house, and sometimes Cruz and Jared had thrown them bits of bread. But I could not catch a chipmunk or a squirrel; they were much too quick for me, and they climbed trees so fast they nearly flew, like birds. By my second day in the woods, I was so hungry that I ate snails I picked from the wet leaves at the base of a tree, and some grubs I found by overturning a rock with my paws and muzzle, but the grubs were bitter and made my stomach ache. There was no standing water to be found in the woods. I was able to lick moisture from leaves and occasionally to lap it from a puddle formed by the endless, misting rain. Early the next morning, awaking cold, bones aching, from a restless night spent listening for the sound of Harold's car, I realized he did not mean to come back.

He'd said as much, but I thought that maybe he would forgive whatever I had done, so I waited as long as I could. An afternoon, a night, that long, hungry day, and most of another night. I have a thick coat, but eventually the drizzle found me and I began to cough, a hoarse barking sound that made my dry throat hurt. Finally, weaker from thirst than from hunger, I made my way to the road and began walking. I was unaccustomed to asphalt, and although it was pleasantly warm from the sun, my pads became sore quickly, and I knew I was limping on that old front leg injury. A truck passed, honking for me to move out of the way, but though I turned and barked, it did not stop. Another car passed, slowed, and nearly stopped. I bounded toward the car, barking with joy and excitement, thinking the occupants might open the door and let me in, but as I ran toward the car, it took off, spattering me with muddy water, leaving me alone again.

⌘ ⌘ ⌘

"Here, boy. Come here, fellow. Come on." I did not trust the false, too-hearty voice of the man who called to me. He had that bitter smell Michael had had sometimes, a chemical odor from something that men like to drink that makes their breath and perspiration stink, and makes them act strangely—sometimes loud and jovial, sometimes cruel, sometimes sorrowful in a way no dog can comfort.

This man smelled like that, but he also smelled like food and like the warm cabin of the truck he called to me from. The evening was cold and the rain had not let up but now was blown sideways by the wind, stinging my eyes and nose. There was only the one man, and I thought that if he tried to harm me I would be able to get away. I approached slowly.

"Come on, dog," Bitter Man called again, and I could hear the impatience in his voice, the growing frustration with my wariness, but I also sensed eagerness and a kind of happy anticipation that allayed my fear.

As I reached the open cab of the truck, Bitter Man gave me a bit of hamburger and it was impossibly delicious—cold but greasy and salty, sweet with blood and catsup, satisfying in a way that kibble can never be. I gulped it and licked his hand, asking for more. He laughed and fastened a leather collar around my neck. I tolerated it, smelling more hamburger in the cab and on his fingers. The collar had metal studs all around, and it was a bit tight over my thick, sodden fur. Bitter Man snapped a leash onto the collar. He pulled the leash harder than he needed to—I would have followed willingly—and half led, half dragged me around to the back of the truck. I knew now that I'd made a mistake, and I struggled, trying to break away from him, but he lowered the tailgate of his truck and yanked on my neck until I leapt in. Then he fastened my leash to a bolt in the side of the truck bed and slammed the tailgate closed. I scrambled for purchase on the slippery metal as he took off into the night.

# Same Cell, Same Smell

I would have followed Bitter Man willingly if he would have given me the chance, even though I disliked him and dreaded whatever was to come. He had me on a chain, so there was no point to struggling. But he did not give me a chance to follow, dragging me down a short flight of steps before I could get steady on my feet after the rough, wet ride in the back of the truck.

As I stumbled, he cursed and yanked the chain again. Scrambling for footing, I saw a girl watching us from a window one flight above the street. She had long, light brown hair and although her eyes were too shadowed to see in the dim illumination provided by the streetlight, I sensed sadness and softness in her.

The next day that same girl brought me a plate of food, but no water, which I needed desperately. My mouth was cracked and sore, and my tongue felt as though it was swollen and sticking to the roof of my mouth. I had nowhere to relieve myself, but at least I was dry, finally, and warm enough. The girl seemed frightened by me, though I treated her politely and moved slowly and carefully, respecting her fear.

The boy who accompanied her the next day was soft-spoken and gentle. I had begun to think I could trust him when Bitter Man returned with another man, this one with a hoarse, raspy voice and a vile odor.

I realized later the young man had been not attacking me but trying to protect me from Rasp-Voice's fierce kick. But in that moment when I bit him, the girl's cry, the men's laughter, and my exhaustion and thirst and fear made me crazy and I snarled and leapt.

The next day Rasp-Voice took me from that basement. I hoped I would never see it again. I had no way to know that what was coming was worse.

Rasp-Voice hoisted me up into the cab of his truck by the chain he had snapped onto my collar. I sat there for a moment, trying to get my bearings, and I must have looked too dazed and exhausted to worry much about, because Rasp-Voice turned, without shutting the door all the way, and went to say something to Bitter Man, the one who had found me on the road.

I saw my chance. Trembling with fear and excitement in equal quantities, I looked around slyly for just a moment, then pushed the door open and dropped to the ground. A shock of pain traveled up my right leg, but I ignored it and took off, the metal chain attached to my collar clanking against the ground and slowing me down unbearably.

Rasp-Voice shouted and took off after me, and for just a moment he was close behind. His foot slammed hard on my chain and brought me up short, choking me, but I turned, snarling against the short chain, and leapt at him. He cursed and jumped back and the chain was free. I took off again, and this time no one could have caught me. Leg throbbing, throat aching, I was intoxicated with freedom and relief as I raced into the night.

⌗ ⌗ ⌗

"Come on, honey," the woman coaxed. "Come on. I'm not gonna hurt you."

I sensed that it was true; her voice and manner were gentle and patient. When I would not come to her, she went to her car, got a dish and jug and poured a bowl of water for me, then backed away respectfully so that I could drink.

Nothing has ever tasted so good as that cool water against my bruised throat.

"Come on, fella. Let me just look at your tags. Somebody must be missing you."

I hesitated. The last time I had trusted a human it had not gone well. But I had few options. I had tried and tried to slip free from the collar, but it was too tight. With the chain clanking behind me, I was too noisy to even hope of catching prey, too noisy even to creep into yards after dark and eat from garbage cans or front porch food bowls.

The woman waited, and finally I relented. Crouching low to the ground, I approached her, and when I'd reached her, instead of grabbing me, she put out her hand politely so that I could smell it. Then she petted my muzzle and scratched around my ears. When she slipped her finger beneath my collar, she cursed.

"Damn it, who would put this on so tight? I'm surprised you can breathe. And there's no tags."

She stood, speaking softly, waiting for me to follow, and finally I did. When she opened the back seat of her big car, I leapt in, sniffing deeply the good smells of human sweat, dog, and children. There was no scent of terror or violence here, just the daily smells of humans and animals going about their business. I sighed, circled, and lay down. I wished with all my heart that she might keep me, but soon enough the car stopped and we were in the parking lot of a familiar building.

⌘ ⌘ ⌘

The Gentle Man unfastened the collar, and I licked his hand gratefully. He slipped a nylon loop around my neck instead and patted my flanks.

"Someone must own him," the woman said. "He had that broken chain on his collar. But it was so tight. And no tags—I don't think he came from a good home."

"I think I know this dog," the Gentle Man said. "I think he mighta come here, oh, five, six years ago. Can't remember, but I think he was adopted." He crouched and ran his hands along my flanks and legs. Then he put a small metal wand near my head. It did not hurt. "No chip. He's been getting fed regular, at least. Maybe not the past few days, but in general."

The woman's voice was thick with sorrow. "I wish I could keep him, but

I've got two dogs already. I can't afford another, especially a big dog like him."

The man got up. "You did the right thing," he said. "He's better off here than on the street. If his owners don't show up, somebody else might take him."

"Good-bye, Big Dog," the woman said. Her voice was falsely bright, not disguising the sorrow beneath her words.

She walked out of my life, and the Gentle Man led me through the familiar front room to the back. Same cell, same smell. I was right back where I'd been before Alfie came into my life, though in that time Alfie had grown from boy to man. The dogs were different, but they were also the same. I did not get to know any of the other dogs this time. After three days of rest and kibble, I was offered for adoption and that very day was taken to my new home.

# Another Kind of Bad Dog

They called me "Big and Bad," as if it were my name, but they said it in a strange, admiring voice, as if *Bad* were something to be proud of. There was little affection in this new place, but there was company: Audrey, a mean-spirited pit bull who prowled the grounds by night and spent her days curled in a cardboard box, snoring, and a loud-voiced, sharp-eared Chihuahua with just three legs they called JuJuBee. We were all guard dogs; our job was not to be petted or to protect our people but simply to warn off intruders at night with our barking, and to punish them, if necessary, should they broach the security of the chained fence that surrounded our store and parking lot.

There was plenty of food, though it was just dry kibble and occasional sandwich scraps, and I enjoyed having other dogs nearby. The pit bull mostly ignored me, and certainly would not let me lie against her by day, snug as she was in her cardboard box, but sometimes in cool weather the Chihuahua would come and curl against me, burrowing into the thick fur at my belly, and I'd sigh and dream about fetch and treats and warm bars of sunlight across a dappled wood floor, and always, always, about my lost boys, both of them.

In all the time I was with Audrey and JuJuBee, we never caught an intruder, but we warned off plenty of them, boys with sticks they smacked along the chain link, laughing and trying to taunt JuJuBee into hurling herself against the fence, howling, and men who fumbled at the padlock on the gate at night, until JuJuBee's sharp ears caught the sound and summoned Audrey and me to come running. Once, leaping into the air to snap at a man's hand as he struggled to climb down, having changed his mind about invading our property, I knocked against Audrey's lean flank and she turned and snapped at me, and I growled back, unaccustomed as I was to other dogs. Audrey grinned and turned, seeming to consider me with her bright, narrow eyes, and though I was the only male in the pack, and a bit larger than Audrey, I wisely cowered and play bowed until her ears went soft again and her strange, stout bowlegs relaxed.

JuJuBee had disappeared at the first sign of trouble, but that night she came and pressed against me, shaking, until we were both still.

## CHAPTER NINE

# *Candy and Carlos*

You would not think four or five kids crowding around you in a public place would be conducive to romance, but somehow it was. All the next week, Carlos would meet me near the high school and we'd pick the kids up together, the twins and four of the Gomez kids, or just Ana and Vittoria, if Miguel and Oscar had T-ball. Then we'd head to the park, the kids happy and excited despite the early dusk.

The first time Carlos took my hand, it might have been an accident. We were walking close together, because Vittoria was on one side of me, clinging to my right hand, and Ana was on Carlos's other side, holding his left. The four boys ran ahead, shouting and falling down and poking each other with sticks, while Carlos laughed and I called out warnings. Ana and Vittoria walked primly beside us, making little sounds of disapproval. Oscar saw Justin on the ground and ran toward him, clearly about to pounce, and I yelled, imagining cracked heads and blood on concrete, but before the words could come out the boys were rolling on someone's dry grass lawn, laughing, everyone fine. I let my hand fall back down to my side and I guess it kind of bumped into Carlos's hand, but instead of ignoring it or cracking a joke, he caught my hand and kept it, lacing his fingers between mine. The girls, bossy and observant as they were, didn't notice a thing, or so I thought.

Carlos didn't look at me and I didn't look at him, but I was completely aware of him, of his size—just a couple of inches taller than me, but broader and heavier across the shoulders, although he was a pretty skinny guy—and of his smell, very faint, like laundry soap and toothpaste. I could feel the rhythm of his steps beside me, but I felt jerky and awkward, as if I'd somehow forgotten how to walk and breathe at the same time.

I worried that my palms might be sweating, and that I might not smell as fresh and soapy as Carlos. I worried that he might notice the bizarre, marionette way I was suddenly walking. I worried that he might not have wanted to hold hands with me; maybe he'd thought *I* was trying to hold hands with *him*. I worried that this moment might somehow end, instead of going on and on forever.

CHAPTER TEN

# A Word from Mom

Do you believe people can come to you in a dream, that people who are no longer living can send you messages from wherever they are, while you are sleeping? Well, I don't. But the dream was so real that I woke at 2:00 a.m. with my fists clenched at my cheeks, pillow wet with tears.

My mother, dressed in her worn jeans and an old plaid shirt that I'd loved to snuggle up against, breathing deeply her smell of Dial soap and Kool Lights and breath mints and this cheap but delicious-smelling lemon shampoo she managed to find wherever we were living. My mother was standing at the edge of my bed with her hand light on my ankle, and I could feel her, I could smell her fragrance, I could hear her soft, slightly hoarse voice, and that's what made me cry, because even in the dream, I knew she was dead, and I realized that until that moment, I had forgotten what my mother's voice sounded like.

"Candy," Mom said gently. "Be a good girl, hear me?"

Oh, Mom. All the way from the grave to give me a message, and that's it? *Be a good girl?* I stayed curled up and still for a long time, eyes closed, because as long as I did, I could still feel her hand on my ankle, I could still hear her soft, slightly throaty voice.

## CHAPTER ELEVEN

# How My Dad Guaranteed that I Will Never Touch a Drop of Alcohol up to and Including the Day I Die

Carlos and I had been at the park, talking. I was a little bummed; he'd caught me in a lie. The thing is, he asked me how come I didn't go to school, and instead of just giving a straight answer, I'd tried to deny it. He'd just sat there, looking at me with this kind of disappointed look on his face and for some reason it had started to really, really piss me off.

I don't know why I couldn't just tell him the truth; I'd never hated school. I'd always kind of liked English, and math came ridiculously easy to me, judging by how much everybody else complained about it. Didn't care for history or chemistry, so sue me. Didn't care for the stupid rules and dress codes and hall passes either, but that's not why I'd bailed. It was just that since my mom had died it had been really hard to get motivated to do much of anything. It had seemed a lot easier not to go than to go. I opened my mouth to explain, but none of that came out.

"What's it to you, Carlos?" I asked, and even I could hear the nasty tone to my voice. "You're not in charge of me. You're not my mother."

That was awkward. Carlos held my gaze for a long time. Then he looked down at his own wiry body and back up at me with a somber expression.

"Sadly, Candy," he said mournfully, "I will never be a mother."

Then we both cracked up, laughing like maniacs, until I fell against him and he froze, and then I froze, and that was kind of awkward too. Then Carlos's arm went around me and I felt—I dunno, calmer, I guess. Just calm and still and somehow lighter inside than I had been. And it occurred to me, the weirdest idea. I was happy.

But does that ever last?

After we walked back to the building and said good night, I went upstairs, still feeling that bouncy, light-inside feeling that was so familiar and unfamiliar at the same time.

I didn't need to use my key; the door was unlocked and open a crack, and as I went inside my nostrils were assaulted by the most hideous stench I've experienced in sixteen years of life—vomit and alcohol and garbage and sweat and I think blood, and maybe even something worse than all of those. My father was not sprawled in his chair, as usual, or even crashed out on the couch. He was flat on his back on the floor, his clothes filthy and his mouth smeared with vomit. A puddle of vomit was on the floor beside his head—partly beneath it, in fact.

He looked dead. I thought about calling 911 and letting an ambulance take him away. Finally I tiptoed to him and touched the side of his neck. I couldn't feel his pulse through the thick folds of his skin, but when I shook him he moaned, so he was alive. I picked up his keys and slipped the truck key off his key ring and onto my own. It wasn't so I could steal his truck, although I'd had a few lessons and could actually drive—unlicensed, but not too badly, all things considered. It was to keep him from waking up and taking off before he was fully sober. He'd done that before.

I thought about leaving, but I couldn't think exactly where to go. I didn't think I could lift my father into the shower. Plus he'd have to go in with his clothes on, and I really didn't want to be there when he came to in a cold shower, fully dressed and probably still wasted.

Finally I stepped around him and opened the window wide. I went in the kitchen and both bedrooms and opened those windows too. Then I cleaned up the vomit with wadded newspaper and damp toilet paper from the bathroom, because we were out of paper towels. I wiped his mouth clean with a damp cloth and kind of pushed him over on his side in case he vomited again.

Then I washed my hands and face and combed my hair, changed my shirt, and went out, locking the door behind me.

I hesitated at the lobby door. It was dark outside. My neighborhood is what you could call colorful by day, kids running around, women pushing shopping carts, and street people bumming change or looking for a place to get out of the sun or the cold, depending on the season. At night it's a different place, still alive, but not in so friendly a way. Our dark streets remind me of an animal that is very, very quiet, but very, very alert, waiting for something. Maybe waiting to get you.

I turned and swallowed hard. I knocked on the Gomezes' door.

# Something Meaner Than Audrey

"Three time loser," the Gentle Man said, laughing, but his laughter was grim as he squatted to rub my head. "You remember me, boy?"

JuJuBee whined and tried edge her way beneath me, but Audrey just sighed, ignoring us both.

"The little Chihuahua wants to stay with the Aussie," the woman who'd brought us in said. "I guess they're friends."

"Okay with me, if it's okay with you, little girl," the man said, turning to take JuJuBee's plastic leash. He sounded tired. "I thought this big guy had a home at last. Shoot, he only been out of here couple months. Lady found him running loose back in December, and he was just about to get put down when he got taken. Thought he was gonna make a good guard dog for the repair shop over on Third."

"Yeah," the woman said. "That's where I got all three of 'em. Place must've gone out of business, and when they left they didn't take the dogs. Just left 'em there, roaming the parking lot. Kids next door were throwing them dinner scraps every night. The pit scared the heck out of the mailman when he tried to deliver a package. I guess they used to keep the dogs inside by day and let 'em roam at night."

"Pit's got some scars on 'er," the Gentle Man observed. "Got tore up in a fight maybe."

A wave of distress rolled off the woman, so pungent my nostrils burned. "Poor old girl," she said. "She didn't actually bite the mailman, you know. Just scared him, I think."

The man shrugged. "You know what gotta be done. Nobody gonna take a pit bull with fight scars and a evil disposition."

JuJuBee pressed against my hind leg, shaking. She looked very small here, in this gleaming white room, and shabbier than she had at the lot, with her bald patches and missing leg.

Audrey didn't look at either of us, nor at the humans. She simply stood, her beautiful sleek head high, her flanks thin but perfectly steady, not trembling. I don't know if Audrey had been in this place before, but I guessed she had, for she displayed no curiosity, no hunger, no anticipation, no fear. She seemed burdened by something heavy and oppressive; a knowledge, I think, of what happened to dogs like her in a place like this. Perhaps when she'd been younger, her coat smoother, her disposition gentler, there'd been a chance for her, but now she was simply an old pit bull bitch; beautiful, still, in her sinister fashion, but not a dog a human might imagine cuddled up before the fire, guarding the front door or pacing protectively by the baby stroller.

When the man led JuJuBee and me away, I hesitated, whining, trying to signal somehow that Audrey belonged with us, but she simply met my eyes with her unwavering gaze, unblinking, until the man tugged at the plastic loop around my neck, forcing me to follow.

I never saw Audrey again, never heard her fearsome bark or the swift pad of her feet on cement.

## CHAPTER TWELVE

# Hot Coffee and a Warm Bed

Mrs. Gomez microwaved me a cup of instant decaf and set it down. I don't usually drink coffee, but I was embarrassed to say so, and when she nudged the cup toward me, I wrapped my cold hands around it, and I had to admit, it felt pretty good. It was bitter as anything, and I inhaled deeply, letting the acrid aroma burn the vomit smell out of my nostrils. The Mexican wedding cookies she set before me on a painted plate were crumbly and sweet. In all the time we'd lived in the building, I'd thought of the super and his wife as "Rafael and Luisa," but now, sitting in their kitchen at their table drinking their coffee, that seemed disrespectful.

The littler kids had gone to bed, but Oscar was still doing homework at the table. He barely looked up when I sat down, just gave me a shy smile and went back to his multiplication. Carlos came into the room and put his arm around his aunt and kissed her forehead, hardly glancing at me, bless his tactful soul. He had his own textbook and a pad of graph paper, but instead of working, he sat with me while his aunt made another cup of coffee. Then she sat down too, taking a cookie for herself while scooting the plate away from Oscar.

"Go on to bed, *mijo*," she told him. "Brush your teeth and I'll wake you early in the morning to finish *la tarea*." She smiled at me, tired lines crinkling the skin around her eyes. "They give him so much homework! He's up sometimes until midnight trying to finish."

Oscar looked at me, fear in his eyes, as if worried that I might say something about his lazy afternoons roughhousing with Justin and Dylan at the park. I shook my head very slightly and he grinned. It was strange to see Carlos there at the table in his T-shirt, without the black hoodie for once. He seemed younger somehow.

When Oscar had gone, Mrs. Gomez put her hand over mine. "You sleep with Ana," she said firmly. She shot Carlos a hard glance and he blushed and looked down at his cup. "I make a place for Vittoria on the floor."

I started to protest but I felt so tired. I hadn't meant to stay the night; I'd just wanted to be somewhere clean and warm and normal for a few minutes. It occurred to me that Mrs. Gomez hadn't asked me a thing. Not why was I here, not did I want to stay the night. I wondered what she might have heard from upstairs before Carlos and I came in. My face got hot. But there was no time to sort through my feelings or talk them over with Carlos. We were all tired, Carlos had homework, and it was time for the rest of the household to go to bed. I followed Mrs. Gomez down the cramped hall to a dark bedroom where three or four kids lay sleeping. She placed a thick folded blanket on the floor and lifted Vittoria onto it as if the little girl weighed nothing. Then she patted the warm spot beside Ana.

"Bathroom next door, just leave the little light on in case Miguel get up," she whispered. She looked at me for a moment, then smoothed my hair with her rough hand. "Sleep well," she said quietly. I thought for a strange, nervous moment that Mrs. Gomez was going to hug me. Instead, she glanced around at her sleeping children with a pleased, tired smile. Then she tiptoed out of the room.

BEAR TWELVE

## *JuJuBee's Mistake*

It wasn't so bad, really, to be back in my pen with a blanket and a bowl of kibble, all the fresh water we wanted, and JuJuBee for company. But she didn't seem to understand this was a temporary place and that she needed to make herself appealing so that we could find a home. I wouldn't have minded if she'd found a place without me; small dogs are more in demand than big ones. Even with two walks a day, I felt the results of being penned up in my hips and knees; I had a restless feeling, a need to run and hunt and roam, that JuJuBee didn't seem to experience. She wanted only to curl against me, taking far more than her share of the little blanket, and when I got up, she got up with me, nervously pacing until I lay back down again.

Sometimes people walked by our pen and exclaimed at the sight of us; a big shaggy dog with matted fur but well muscled, and with eyes that I imagined were still clear and bright, and a three-legged Chihuahua who couldn't have weighed more than seven or eight pounds even after a month of steady feedings. When someone stopped, amused by our friendship, I'd nudge JuJuBee to get up and go the wire and say hello, to lick their fingers or wag her tail, but she would only shiver and snuggle close to me, distressed and miserable.

The Gentle Man tried separating us, but JuJuBee sat huddled in the back of her box, crying softly, and so he put us back together, but his words were chilling. I knew their significance, even if JuJuBee did not.

"Little girl, you got to perk up and find a home," he told her softly, patting her trembling flanks. "We can't keep you here forever. You a cute dog, but they a lot of cute dogs, and most of 'em got four legs and a friendlier disposition."

And so I knew, not three days later, when the blue-haired Death Girl

64

walked by our pen, hesitated, and turned back again, sighing, that either JuJuBee or I, or perhaps both of us, was marked for a visit to the room behind the gray wall.

I nudged JuJuBee to standing as the girl worked at the latch on our pen. JuJuBee tried to hide beneath me, but I pushed her impatiently, trying to signal my plan. A swift glance through the holding room door toward the lobby told me the heavy glass front doors were closed, but there was a couple crossing the parking lot, and if I timed it right, we might have a chance.

When the door swung open, I hesitated, so that the girl had to take a step into the pen to reach for JuJuBee. My stomach sick with dread, I leapt into the air, crashing against the girl with my full weight, more than enough to knock her down, and she shrieked and fell against the mesh side of the enclosure. JuJuBee was shaking harder than I'd ever seen her, a yellow puddle growing beneath her where she had disgraced herself. The couple were nearly at the door, and as they pushed it open, I seized JuJuBee in my jaws, gently as I could, and streaked through the holding room, into the lobby, and out the front door just as the man was holding the door for the lady.

Shouts, screams, a curse, a woman's hysterical laughter, hot asphalt beneath my paws, JuJuBee squirming in my mouth, hot sun above, busy street beyond the hedges. I spun, looking for the best way out. The Gentle Man came out of the building, plastic leash in one hand, broom handle in the other. I tossed JuJuBee down as gently as I could and barked a swift command and we ran together, then, like wild dogs, a pack at last, JuJuBee's three legs pumping as if her very life depended on them. And I guess they did.

⌗ ⌗ ⌗

It was JuJuBee who identified the safe spot first, a dark corner just inside an alley; the back door of some business that seemed to have been closed forever, with trash piled up against the wall. An abandoned shopping cart was parked in the shadows, piled high with clothes and blankets and a tantalizing fragrance that I thought might be hamburger grease. I sniffed cautiously, wondering why the area smelled so strongly of humans when we were the only living thing in sight, but JuJuBee hopped right up onto the doorstep, sighed, and lay down. She had to be exhausted; we'd run the same distance, but I'd done it on four strong legs much longer than her three.

What I needed most was a drink of water. I'd eaten breakfast that morning, but I usually waited until the Gentle Man freshened the water bowls before I had a drink, so I'd gone without, and the dry kibble followed by the frantic run had left me panting. JuJuBee seemed in better shape. Her sides were barely heaving now, and she looked comfortable stretched out on the stone step. I touched her gently with my nose before I made my way down the dark alley, searching for water.

## CHAPTER THIRTEEN

# *Where You From?*

Things at home were bad.

My dad wouldn't even try to go out and get work anymore. I'd kept his truck key, but he must've had an extra. It hardly mattered—he just drove down the block, for beer and smokes. Mostly he sat in his chair, shouting things at the TV. When there was food in the house, it was what I bought with babysitting money—cheap stuff that stretches, like pasta and peanut butter and jelly. But I could never get my dad to eat. As his arms and legs got skinnier and saggier looking, his belly got bigger, bulging out over his waistband like somebody had tucked a basketball under his shirt.

Once in a while, Carlos would knock on the door with a covered dish from his aunt, enchiladas or Mexican lasagna or just a big bowl of beans and rice. Carlos would act like he hardly knew me, muttering something like, "Uh, my aunt said to bring this up to your dad so he can try some authentic Mexican food." I'd try to catch his eye or touch his hand while I was taking the dish, but Carlos never let his guard down. I thought that he might be a little afraid of my dad, or maybe he was ashamed of himself, for what we'd been doing.

Don't get all worked up; we hadn't been doing much except sneaking around a little. I was sixteen, and the only time I'd been to second base was playing softball in PE. But we'd kissed a few times, first just a dry peck on the lips, then a deeper, slower, wetter kiss that had made me extremely conscious of Carlos's shoulder and thigh pressed against mine as we sat on a bench at the park, huddled together against the dark.

The same dark that made it private and romantic made it dangerous too. A couple of times thugs wandered by and gave us the eye, and more than a couple of times drunks stumbled past, making remarks. The drunks didn't bother us, but the thugs did. The first time two of them sauntered by, Carlos pulled me very close to him and grew very still. I could feel him straining to listen as the bangers disappeared into the shadows. They were only kids, not as old as Carlos or even as old as me, but I felt a sick, slow turn in my stomach when Carlos put his face close to my ear and whispered, "If anything goes down, get out of here. Run down to the 7-11 and call for help."

I nodded, but nothing happened; the thugs had gone. I wondered if I would have done what he'd said, if they had attacked us or harassed us. I think I would have stayed to fight. I am a girl, and I am no gangster, but it would still have been two against two so Carlos could have had a chance.

The second time bangers checked us out was scarier. It was Valentine's Day; not a big deal, but I had made Carlos brownies and he had gotten me . . . drum roll. Not a ring, not a necklace, not even flowers. He had gotten me a book, and because he was my first boyfriend, if that's even what he was, I will admit I had hoped for something the teeniest bit more romantic than a paperback: *Zen and the Art of Motorcycle Maintenance*. "It's . . . You'll see," Carlos explained, or didn't explain, I guess. I was trying not to act disappointed. "You're my Chautauqua," he said, and then I couldn't wait to get home and start reading, to find out exactly what that could possibly mean. "When I'm with you, I think about things. I think about the future, about the stuff I want to get out of life, you know?"

I loved watching Carlos talk. When he got really serious, he had this way of worrying his lip with his teeth. Watching him do that made me want to kiss his mouth, but I also wanted to hear what he was saying, especially since it was about me.

"I never told you this," Carlos said, "but the reason I came here? I got into some trouble. I didn't do anything, but I had to get away from my high school. It was . . . You know, where I come from, the schools are kind of rough."

I laughed. Where I come from, the schools are kind of rough too. I thought he knew that.

"So I got my equivalency," he said. "I never really graduated. But Tía

Luisa let me come here, so I could get some college classes handled and try to get my grades up high enough for a scholarship, you know?"

I nodded. I hadn't actually known you could go to college without graduating from high school. That was a fairly interesting idea, although I wasn't completely sure I'd be going to college. We were sitting on our usual bench beneath a graceful jacaranda tree, and dusk had sneaked up on us. The night was a little cool; the days were growing longer, with long twilights that seemed almost endless. Carlos had given me his sweatshirt, smelling of soap and mint. I thought about what he was saying. This somewhat explained why even though Carlos's grades were really good, he was hell-bent on straight As—thus the late night algebra tutorials. I'd breezed through geometry freshman year; math has always been easy for me. If I'd showed up for sophomore year, I'd have been halfway through Algebra II. Sometimes when I thought about that, I felt a sick, scared tug in my stomach. What was I doing? I couldn't just pretend to go to school forever; someday I'd have to graduate or not graduate, and if it was not, that would make me one of the dread tribe High School Dropout.

Carlos was saying something about trying for a scholarship back home in New Mexico, and I was watching his mouth and wishing he'd kiss me and worrying about not going to school and feeling a little cold despite the sweatshirt, when a car pulled up on the side street off the main drag, maybe thirty feet from us. It was a big four-door sedan. The driver's side front and back windows eased down, and I felt Carlos stiffen beside me.

"Candy, get up real casual, and just walk away," Carlos said in a calm voice, as the driver looked over at us. I knew better than to argue, but I didn't get up either. It was like watching a TV show where everything is ordinary, but you know something bad is about to go down. I felt my blood pounding in my temple. Carlos pulled his hand away from mine. "Go, on, Candy," he said gently. "I don't think they're gonna bother you."

The driver called out then. "Hey, man, where you from?"

It sounded friendly enough, but if you're from L.A., even if you're white, even if you're wealthy, even if you live in a mansion in a gated community at the top of Bel Air Crest and the closest you ever got to gangbanging was watching a roundup on the evening news, even then you know that there's no good answer to that question, because wherever you are from, if you are young and male and black or brown, you are somebody's sworn enemy. Without even knowing you, somebody hates you enough to kill you, just based on whatever the answer to that question might be.

Carlos didn't answer. The jacaranda leaves whispered as a breeze drifted over from the ocean. I heard Carlos breathing, I heard the car idling, I heard a child crying a few blocks away. A dog barked somewhere. Traffic moved around us, cars speeding by on the main boulevard. Something moved within the dark confines of the back seat of the car, and I saw the gleam of metal and heard a man's voice—a boy's voice, really, low and full of urgency.

The driver called again. "Where you from, homes?"

Two things happened in that moment, both amazing. The first was that behind the sedan, another car turned the corner from the main boulevard and rolled past slowly. For a second it was just a car, a black nose emerging from the dark shadows of the trees, and then I saw the white sides and the unlit red dome; the po-po, the 4-0. Yes, a police patrol car, and I couldn't have been happier if Superman had swooped down from Gotham or Metropolis or wherever he hangs out when he's not rescuing people. The cops didn't do anything but switch on the cherry light, but that was enough to get the sedan moving along its way.

The other thing that happened was that just at that moment, right when the driver called out for the second time, just before the cruiser turned the corner and maybe saved our lives, just at that moment, Carlos said in a low, sad voice, "Candy, whatever happens, I love you."

# BEAR THIRTEEN

## *JuJuBee Makes a Friend*

Belly full of water I'd lapped from a backyard birdbath, I made my way back toward the doorstep where I'd left JuJuBee. Halfway up the alley I froze, hearing a human voice, low and even. It was a man speaking, but his voice reminded me of Jocelyn's from long ago, the way she'd sounded at night when she was reading Jared a story. It had been one of my favorite times, the near-end of every busy day, Cruz gone home, Michael downstairs reading his paper, and the three of us safe and warm and tired upstairs, mother and son wedged into the rocking chair and me at their feet on Jared's braided rug, chin resting on Jocelyn's warm shoe.

The man's voice was a steady murmur. There was no smell of fear or anger drifting down the alley, just a stronger fragrance of hamburger now, and JuJuBee's scent, and a somewhat pleasing odor of unwashed human.

He sat on the step, hardly more than a boy, dressed in bulky layers of dirty clothes that made him seem larger than he really was. His wrists and ankles were skinny and pale. He held a bit of hamburger for JuJuBee, who stood pressed against his leg, waiting respectfully as he tore off bits of meat and offered them to her.

"That's a girl," the man chanted softly, over and over. "Good girl, good dog, so hungry. Here's a little more. Poor girl, so hungry."

She couldn't have been that hungry; she'd eaten kibble with me only that morning, but the grease and meat smelled delicious, and the sight of the man's hand, gently stroking JuJuBee's back, made my own skin tingle with longing and loneliness.

"Good girl," the man said again. "Want to come up?" He patted his lap. I smelled fear from JuJuBee, but longing too, even greater than my own. The man waited patiently, and at last JuJuBee shivered all over and leapt,

71

scrabbling for purchase with her three paws until the man's strong arm went around her, gently steadying her. JuJuBee settled into his lap and he went back to stroking her behind the ears and along her neck, stopping now and then to feed her a bit of meat, then take a bite for himself.

I watched, fascinated. Surely JuJuBee knew I was there; she could hear and smell at least as well as I, but she ignored me, curled on the man's lap as if she'd been there her whole life. I crept closer, nearly shuddering with longing—for the meat or for the petting, I don't know. Both, I suppose.

"Good girl," the man said. "You're safe now. Good dog."

I sighed then, and I suppose even his weak human ears could not help but hear me. He froze, looking up with wide eyes, frightened, I think, but wary and ready to fight too. JuJuBee leapt off his lap and faced me, growling softly. Then she seemed to remember herself and she came toward me, whining respectfully.

"Who's this?" the man said softly. "Have you got a friend, little one?"

I moved a little closer to them, slowly, knowing my large size could easily frighten a human into rash action.

"Hey, boy. You hungry too? I don't have much left, but you can have a bite." He threw the last bit of hamburger bun into the air and I whirled to catch it before it hit the ground, the delectable smell of grease filling my muzzle even as I gulped the bite down. I was hungrier than I'd thought, and when the man got up and went to the shopping cart, I waited expectantly. Finally he poured a handful of cereal on the ground for me, and then put a bit in his palm for JuJuBee, who ate unhesitatingly.

The cereal was sweet and crunchy, but I ate warily, finally settling down near JuJuBee and the man, but not within arm's reach of him. JuJuBee herself had no reservations. When he unfolded a flattened cardboard box and spread a blanket over it, she curled up beside him, nestled against his chest as if she'd been there her whole life.

## CHAPTER FOURTEEN

# *Not Just Romance and Horror*

When you have been in danger, and then you are safe, the world takes on a perfect crystal clarity. Walking home with Carlos Valentine's night, clasped hands swinging between us, we were alert to every sound because we weren't sure the bangers wouldn't try to find us, but also, in my case at least, because I felt perfectly and completely alive in a way I had not felt for a long time.

It hurt when my mom died, of course. It hurt when my dad starting caring more about his next beer than he did about me. It hurt that nobody but Carlos seemed to notice or care that I wasn't going to school, not my dad, not my old classmates, not my teachers from freshman year. But it hurt in a weird way, like I was wrapped in a cocoon of cotton, in a blanket, so that nothing could really hit me with full impact, but nothing could make me really happy or delighted or excited either. Well, that was over. The cocoon had fallen away, and I'm not sure whether I was a butterfly or a moth, but I was alive and happy and beautiful and very ready to stretch my wings.

I waited for Carlos to say something about what had happened—the thugs, the cops, and especially the "I love you"—but he didn't. He just held my hand tightly and walked along, and when we got close to the building, he pulled me into a darkened doorway and put both arms around me. I put my head on his shoulder and let myself relax, and it felt so good to lean on another person like that, to be held in someone's arms. I realized that my dad had not actually put his arms around me a single time since my mom had died, and she had been too weak to do much hugging for a long time before that. This hug made me feel protected and cherished and safe.

Finally Carlos pulled away. I turned my face up to his. I thought he would kiss me, but he didn't. He just looked at me, for a long, long time.

"I'm here to see my guidance counselor," I told the receptionist. "I think it's still Mr. Redmond."

She looked at me vaguely through greasy glasses, blinking as if the tepid fluorescent light was too much for her. Finally she motioned to the door behind her. "Knock and go in."

I'd only met Mr. Redmond once before. Usually students didn't see the counselor much until junior year, unless they needed a work permit or a recommendation letter for juvie or something. He was a red-faced man with a block-shaped head and a weary expression.

"Oh, yes," Mr. Redmond said as I entered, my knock having been ignored. "You're the one that lost her mother."

I considered several snide responses but finally just nodded. "Candace Scott. Candy. I'm supposed to be . . . I mean, I was a freshman last year."

"And this year?" Mr. Redmond was tracing something on his computer monitor with his finger. "If I'm not mistaken, you transferred out."

I nodded again, relieved. Whatever they'd marked me down as, it didn't seem to be "truant" or "dropout."

"The thing is, Mr. Redmond, I've been attending another school, and . . . it's not working out so well. I'd like to come back to City High."

He peered at me over the top of his thick glasses. "Where are you currently? Which high school?"

I didn't answer, and he fidgeted impatiently. "I'll need your records, Miss Scott. Transcripts with grades. You can have them forwarded electronically, or you can bring hard copies in a sealed envelope."

I shook my head. "I don't actually have transcripts, sir . . . I wasn't actually attending an official school. I was being homeschooled by my dad."

Mr. Redmond nodded. "That's fine. Just send me something in writing indicating where you are in your coursework, subject by subject. What assessments, if any, books read, documentation of any labs if you're taking a science course . . . Whatever you have."

I grinned, hardly believing it was going to be that easy. I'd missed nearly six months of school—most of the year—and if I could keep up with my classmates for the last quarter, I'd finish the year and move on to eleventh grade. I thanked the fates I'd picked some heavy duty stuff out at the library, not just romances and horror, though there'd been some of that sprinkled in between the Jane Austen and Edith Hamilton. And I hadn't imagined the hours spent helping Carlos with algebra would end up helping me as much as him, but now I was thankful I'd kept sharp.

Mr. Redmond gave me a long, appraising look. "Remember to have everything signed off on by whatever credentialed teacher you've had supervising your work," he added.

Bam! That sound you just heard was my heart hitting the floor.

⌘ ⌘ ⌘

When I was a little girl, my mom would always promise we'd go to the beach, but we hardly ever did. It was hard to get around—we lived in the Valley, and then in Koreatown, where I learned what it really and truly means to be an outsider, and then Hollywood. But wherever we lived, my mom and I bussed it if we had to go anywhere. So she'd promise we'd go to the beach, and then something would come up—work, or rain, or maybe just the sheer logistics of bussing it all the way to one of the beach cities.

But we did go once. I guess I was seven or eight. Our landlady at the Koreatown apartment, Mrs. Park, was taking her nephews to the beach for the day, and she invited us to ride along. She had a cooler full of Cokes and sandwiches and this really weird spicy coleslaw stuff that was pretty delicious, and my mom brought a package of cookies and, embarrassingly, a soft, partly crushed loaf of sliced bread.

At the beach, the boys stood timidly at the shore, shrieking and dancing away every time the water rushed close. Mrs. Park spread a blanket, put up a huge striped umbrella, and patted the place beside her, inviting my mother to sit down. But Mom must have seen the longing on my face. Nothing had ever called to me like that cold gray water, foamy and wild, rushing to the sand and pulling away again in all directions at once, full of mystery and promise and danger and beauty. I just stood there, knee deep, my shorts wet to my waist, staring at the water, the waves, the birds that flew in lazy formation against the white sky.

My mom said something and Mrs. Park laughed and called a warning to her nephews, who were in very little danger, having barely wet their toes. Then Mom stepped gingerly to where I waited, took my hand, and together we waded out, the sand like a soft cool bed beneath us, the water teasing and rude and bitterly cold. When the water was at the height of my chin, my mother showed me how to jump up each time a wave rolled toward us so that it could lift and carry me, letting me roll with it and be part of it before it crashed against the shore.

Eventually Mrs. Park called us to lunch and we came out of the water reluctantly. I was so cold that my body shook uncontrollably and my teeth chattered. My mother held me on her lap beneath our towel, trying to warm me with her own cold body. Mrs. Park wrapped us in the picnic blanket, fussing under her breath as the boys watched, solemnly, probably wondering if I was going to die. I wouldn't have minded. It was the happiest day of my entire life. I think it might still be. That was when I got the little piece of sea glass I always keep with me, for luck. I was looking for shells there in the wet sand, right before we had to go, and there weren't any. But then a wave pulled back and my mom bent over and picked a little blob of pale blue glass worn smooth by the sea. It looked like a cloud that had dropped from the sky.

We promised each other a dozen times, but my mother and I never made it back to the beach together, not even when we lived in Santa Monica, less than two miles from the pier. We meant to, but I had school, and then she never had time, and then when she did have time, she was too sick to go to the water. I go there a lot, by myself, now. In summer I jump waves and body surf, but when the weather's cold, I just sit and think about things. Sometimes I think about my mom wading right into that freezing water with me, my hand safe in hers. How many moms would do that?

I miss my mother so much. I don't think about how much I miss her very often, because — and I know I suck, okay? But sometimes I'm really, really mad at her. I love her and all. But I'm still mad.

# Something That Had Been Cold for a Long Time

I didn't have anything against him, but he was JuJuBee's human, that was clear. I slept near them in the alley, most nights, and I walked along behind them, sometimes, as they made the rounds, hunting for good things to eat and cans the man could trade in for money if he collected enough of them. When he had enough, he'd share with me too, offering me half of a sandwich or the last bit of a melted ice cream cone, but he belonged to JuJuBee and she to him. Somewhere the man had found a thin leather collar, small but still too big for JuJuBee, and he'd spent an hour punching a new hole in the collar and sawing off the extra leather before he fastened it around her neck. A tiny silver-colored heart hung down from the collar, and if JuJuBee moved quickly, it jingled. The noise wasn't unpleasant, but I didn't envy her the collar, though I would have enjoyed the leftover bit of leather he handed JuJuBee to chew. It smelled delicious and reminded me of the bones Cruz and Jocelyn had once saved for me after the family had enjoyed a steak.

I was happy for JuJuBee, but I needed to find a place of my own. I even thought with longing of Audrey's fierce grin and swift paws. There were times nothing can make a dog feel safer than to be side by side with another dog, smelling and hearing her cues, acting in tandem in a way that humans, love them as I do, do not seem to comprehend. JuJuBee had been a tough little girl, but that seemed to have all gone out of her. She was a tired old three-legged dog, spoiled and content to ride in her man's shopping cart or trot close at his heels, or best of all, press beside him on that worn cardboard mat, keeping watch over him as he slept, protected and protecting.

I'd regained some of my muscle during those weeks at the shelter with

JuJuBee but now felt myself grow leaner than ever before; my hip bones began to emerge from the thinning fur at my flanks, and once when I let the man touch my back, I could feel the knobs of my spine against his gentle fingers. But I felt myself growing strangely stronger than I'd been as a well-fed young dog romping with Jared or curled on my hallway rug at Alfie's, stronger than I'd been those long lonely months in my pen at the shelter, well fed but seldom exercised. Now my muscles were sinewy and tough, and it was nothing for me to go a full day without something to eat. Eventually I'd find a pizza crust in the gutter or a discarded loaf of bread under the dumpster at the grocery store, or JuJuBee's human would share with me when JuJuBee had had her fill, picking daintily from his fingers as if she'd been born to a life of ease.

My front leg had never healed right since the beating at Michael's hand; I could run well on it, but I was aware that my gait was somewhat lopsided, and sometimes that made my shoulder on the other side ache. My fur didn't keep me quite as warm as it once had—those last few nights at Alfie's sleeping outdoors I'd been warm and snug in my own skin, with nothing between the ground and me. Now I shivered on a cold morning. But I'd gained a toughness that I enjoyed; when I walked alone, humans gave me wide berth. Other dogs approached cautiously, though most would stop and sniff to say hello, and the braver among them, usually a rottie or pit bull pup on a leash with a nervous human at the other end, might play bow and dance away, inviting me to chase. I never did; my life was about survival now, not play. It was a hard life, but not altogether a bad life for a dog.

One night I felt something warm in me that had been cold for a long time. I had crept close to JuJuBee and her human, my belly full for once with rinds of cheese and delicious tough rolls he had pulled from the supermarket dumpster. It was a cool night, and I let my chin rest on the edge of the folded cardboard, and then, to my surprise, there was the man's hand on my neck, gently stroking my matted fur.

"You're a good old boy," the man said gently. "Yes, you are. You're a good dog, like a big old grumpy bear. That's what I'm going to call you, Bear."

The sound of my true name delighted me and hurt me at the same time. I am not ashamed to say I whined then, like a puppy, and let my tail thump against the cold pavement. I held perfectly still, wishing only for the man to scratch my neck and say my name again, *Bear*. It had been an awfully long time since I had heard my name and those precious words, nearly forgotten: *good dog*.

Then JuJuBee growled low in her throat and leapt to her feet, the man cried out, and I got up fast, facing down whatever it was there at the mouth of the alley that had alerted JuJuBee, not so spoiled after all but beneath her new demeanor as alert to danger as ever, as vigilant in her guardianship of her pack.

# Like a Wounded Bear

There were two humans, a bad smell rolling off them, a smell that lifted the hackles along the back of my ruff and had JuJuBee snarling like a wild creature, even as she trembled hard enough to jangle the little charm on her leather collar. The taller man wore a dirty black coat and had a stick that he poked at JuJuBee while the other one, really just a boy, laughed nervously.

"What'choo got there, man, a little wolf cub?" Black Coat said. His voice dripped with menace. "She's a tough one."

"Leave her alone," JuJuBee's human said bravely, but his thin voice broke and I knew he was afraid. I moved in front of him, side by side with JuJuBee, and let a long, low growl escape my throat.

"Hey, call him off," the Boy said, and the smell grew ranker and sharper, threat now laced with fear.

I growled again and JuJuBee whined softly, under her breath.

"We not gonna hurt you, man," Black Coat told JuJuBee's human. "We only want the dogs. See?" He held up a rope, already knotted into a noose. "We not gonna take your money or nothing."

JuJuBee's man was about to answer when Black Coat moved, quicker than I would have thought possible, and cracked the stick down on my head, hard. I yelped and fell over, stunned, and JuJuBee's man screamed, and JuJuBee barked as the Boy grabbed her and took off down the alley, running. JuJuBee's man went for Black Coat, and I struggled to my feet, my head throbbing and my vision partially obscured by a trickle of hot blood.

JuJuBee's man had one end of the stick but Black Coat had the other, and they fell to the ground, rolling and cursing, neither willing to let go. I heard JuJuBee's shrill howls and took off after the Boy, who cried out as

I threw my body against his back and knocked him flat on the ground. JuJuBee escaped his arms just in time to keep from being crushed. She leapt onto the Boy's back and licked my face, again and again, whining. I ignored her soothing tongue, concentrating on the Boy who lay perfectly still beneath me. The smell of urine and sweat and fear rose off of him, and his breath was thick and labored. When he struggled, I growled and he lay still again.

I waited for JuJuBee's man to arrive and help me, but it was Black Coat I smelled coming down the alley. I gave JuJuBee a sharp, hard bark, commanding her to run to safety if she could, as I leapt off the Boy and whirled to face Black Coat. The heart on JuJuBee's collar tinkled like a tiny bell as she scrambled away, and that was the last thing I heard as a rope tightened around my neck, jerking me off my feet, and the world went silent and black.

# Big and Bad and Chained to a Rail

I expected that they would be beat me, but they didn't. Instead, they gave me a thick blanket to sleep on that was comfortable enough, given that I was tied by a stout rope to the rail on their small balcony, high above the city. It was cold on the balcony, but that helped the cut over my eye stop bleeding and seemed to ease the throbbing in my head.

When the Boy came out with a bowl heaped with canned food and another of water, I looked politely away from him, so that he would feel no threat. He stood and watched as I wolfed the good food, and I felt longing and sorrow and regret seeping from his pores, and shame too.

When Black Coat came out, the Boy hesitated and I smelled courage and fear. "Hey, why don't we keep this one," he said in a high, piping voice. I realized then he was very young, not a near-man like Alfie—perhaps just a few years older than Jared had been.

"We could use him for protection, and to, you know, lure the other dogs so they trust us, you know? He's not a bad dog. He coulda bit me when he had me down, and he didn't."

Black Coat made a harsh, sneering sound deep in his throat. He smacked the Boy lightly on the back of his head with one big hand, a warning.

"Don't get soft, boy," he said roughly. "We got plans for that dog and a bunch more like him."

Black Coat went inside and after a moment, the Boy did too. He came out a few minutes later with a folded newspaper and laid it flat, as far away from my dish as I could reach, tied as I was. I understood that it was for me to use to relieve myself, and much as that repelled me, when it grew dark and no one came to walk me, eventually I had no choice.

The next day Black Coat brought two more dogs out onto the balcony, though only I was tied. They were a pair of beagles, friendly enough, but interested mostly in each other. I could smell anxiety from them, but not real fear. They were well fed and polite, with jangling collars—certainly not street dogs. I wondered how they had fallen into Black Coat's hands. The terrier mix the Boy brought out that night was another matter. He was a young dog, hardly more than a puppy, with a scruffy yellow coat and an injured hind paw that had a bad smell, like pus or rot. He was terrified, shaking in the Boy's arms although the Boy held him gently, speaking softly and stroking his dirt-stiff fur.

There were four of us now on the cramped balcony, and though the terrier and I kept mostly silent, the beagles yapped long and loud. A couple of times people had yelled complaints from neighboring apartments, and then Black Coat would come out and shout and kick the nearest dog, whichever it might be. The Boy brought us food and fresh water and often stopped to stroke the terrier's coat or to let me sniff his hand, though he seemed afraid to pet me. I reassured him as best I could, wondering if we were to stay on this small balcony forever.

On the third or fourth day, the Boy came out and tied lengths of plastic rope to the beagles' collars. He picked the terrier up in his arms, and as the beagles danced with excitement, whining and yelping, Black Coat came and untied me from the rail. I stretched, eager to relieve the cramps that the short leash had caused. Black Coat yanked the rope and dragged me through the living room, though I tried as best I could to follow on stiff legs. We rode silently in the elevator, Black Coat impatient with the tears that the Boy struggled to hold back. I could smell anxiety and sorrow in his sweat. I was somehow grateful for his soothing hand in the little terrier's scruffy fur.

There were two more dogs already in the car, both medium-sized mongrels, one short-haired, and one long. They moved over for me and I sat with my face pressed to the window, the beagles and mutts scrambling for purchase on the slick seat. I think the Boy had intended to hold the terrier on his lap, but before he started the car, Black Coat looked over at him, gave a snort of disgust, and yanked the dog up by the scruff of his neck, tossing him over the seat. He landed on me, but I didn't snap or even move. I let him slip down between my body and the seat, and he rode that way, crying so softly that I'm sure the humans could not hear him, for the duration of the trip.

## CHAPTER FIFTEEN

# A Resounding No

"So I'm supposed to sign off on all this?" Julia asked, exasperated. It had taken me ages to write it all up, the history I'd missed, the math I'd been doing with Carlos almost daily, the books I'd read and a few others I fudged—thank you, free BookRags samples!

"Candy, I can't do anything that's not strictly by the rules. I'd risk my credential."

"You're not doing anything wrong," I argued. "You just have to sign off that I really did all this work, and I did, Julia. Honestly. Any reading I didn't do, I'll catch up on before the end of the year, promise."

She nodded. "But what about science? And foreign language?"

"I can't fake those," I admitted. "But I can make them up in summer school, before eleventh grade. You'll see—it'll work out fine."

The twins' overweight King Charles spaniel waddled in, looking for a handout. It was a somewhat unappealing dog with drooping, red-rimmed eyes and a thick, lopped-off stub of a tail. Julia had told me it was a pure-bred, originally probably very expensive, but someone had stopped loving it, I guess, and had tied it to Julia's front porch railing while she and her husband were at work.

"You can give Sparky a cookie," Julia told me, as if that were some fabulous privilege reserved only for the most fortunate visitors. She took a jar down from the shelf over the table and handed me a hard little biscuit shaped like a bone.

"I'm not much of a dog person," I told her, setting the biscuit on the table.

"Look, here's the other thing," Julia said. She barely flinched at a loud thump and a crash from upstairs.

"Knock it off, boys!" Julia yelled, without getting up. "The thing is," she continued in a normal voice, without missing a beat, "I'm what's called a mandated reporter. All teachers are. It means that if you actually haven't been to school at all this year . . ." She met my eyes to make sure I understood. "If that's what you were *actually* saying, I would have to call Child Protective Services."

I swallowed hard. "I didn't mean *that*," I lied. "I meant I just skipped a few classes . . ." I grabbed the sheaf of papers out of her hands. "Forget it. I've got to go, anyway."

"Look, Candy. It's too bad you have to deal with this now, while you're really just a kid. But some people have to grow up faster than others. That's just the way it is." Julia paused. "There might come a time you have to turn your dad in so you can both get some help. There are places —"

"Are you *crazy*, Julia?" I demanded. "He hasn't done anything! He has some problems, sure, but don't we all?"

Julia gave me a level look. "Just make sure all that loyalty is well deserved, Candy. Because you deserve something too." She got up from the table and went to the fridge. She took out a carton of milk and got some plastic cups down from the cupboard. "Have some milk and fig bars with us before you take off," she said, handing me the milk to pour. "Boys! Come on down, snack time, and Candy's leaving!"

It might seem like my day couldn't get much worse, but somehow, it managed. When I came in, juggling a plate of fig bars in one hand and a foil-wrapped bowl of Julia's yummy rigatoni in the crook of my arm, the apartment was strangely dark. A bit of cold light spilled in from the street, enough for me to make out my dad's outline as he sat slumped in his chair, beer in one fist, chin in the other.

"Why're you sitting here with all the lights out, Dad?" I asked, flipping the switch by the door. Nothing. I made my way to the kitchen, trying not to bang my shins, and set the food down on the dirty counter. No lights in there either. "Did we blow every bulb in the house at the . . ." I faltered. "Dad! Did you forget to pay the electric bill? Our power's off!"

He grunted and took a swig of beer. "Din' forget nothin', dumbass. Din' happen to have a spare hunnerd and eighteen bucks laying around."

"Dad," I said slowly. "I know you haven't been working much . . . but I didn't know things were that bad." A sudden, horrible thought occurred to me. "Have you been paying our *rent*? Are we about to get kicked out of here or something?"

My father shifted in his chair as if he were about to get up. Then he settled back down. Apparently standing up to yell at me was too much trouble. "Don't you take that tone of voice with me, girlie," he said angrily. "'Bout time you started pulling your weight around here."

"Dad, I do," I argued. "I try! I buy food with my babysitting money whenever I can! But you never told me you couldn't pay the electric!"

He shook his head. In the dark, as we were, it was just the sad, slow movement of a misshapen lump. "And I notice you never run out of beer," I added, and instantly regretted it. My father sat upright, threw one arm back, and let fly. I scrambled out of the way, fast, and the beer bottle smacked the china cabinet behind me, breaking the glass and spattering my legs with beer and shards of glass.

"You broke Mom's china cabinet!" I yelled, disbelieving. My voice sounded awful in my own ears as it caught in my throat. I sounded like an animal that had been hurt. I'm not a yeller; never have been. I'm more the "hold a slow, silent grudge for a day or two and then forget about it" type. But he had smashed the glass of the china cabinet that was about the only nice thing my mom had owned. And he had done it throwing a heavy bottle right at me.

I ran to my room, slamming the TV stand with my shin, then banging my hip on the doorframe. I sat down against the door, blocking it with my weight, but I didn't hear anything from the other room. No sound, no movement. My legs were sticky with beer. No blood. After a long time, I reached over and pulled the blanket off the bed and wrapped it around myself. That's how I slept, pressed against the door, praying no cockroaches would crawl into my ears in the night.

## CHAPTER SIXTEEN

# *Unfortunately, My Life Is Not a Movie*

In the movies, a really crappy day like mine would be followed by something utterly wonderful. In real life, it was not.

When I got up, Dad was gone. I cleaned up the mess as much as possible, and cut my thumb on a shard of glass. We didn't have any Band-Aids or even paper towels, so I wrapped my hand in a gigantic wad of toilet paper and fastened it with a piece of Scotch tape. Great look. My sneakers reeked of beer, so I had to wear a pair of my mom's that were an embarrassing shade of electric blue. I knew there was nothing much to eat in the fridge, but when I opened it to check anyway, a nearly empty carton of milk and dried-up dish of rice emitted a damp odor that reminded me that it was going to be another very dark night if we didn't get the power back on.

Carlos was waiting on the stoop when I came down. Fool that I am, when I saw him there, looking sick and worried, I assumed it had to do with the shouting and bottle breaking he'd probably overheard the night before. Little did I know, Carlos had his own plan in mind to completely destroy my day.

"Hey," I said, sitting beside him on the cement stoop. Carlos leaned over and kissed the side of my head. I turned, hoping for something more by way of a lip-lock, but he got up, taking my hand.

"Let's walk, Lemon."

His voice was not teasing at all, though. It was soft and heavy and full of sorrow.

The sun beat down on the tops of our heads and it felt good. The short California winter was coming to a close. It was time for flowers and breezes and birdies and all good things, like, for example, an afternoon on the beach with my bae.

But Carlos wasn't feeling it. He led me to our spot on the bench in the park, sat down, and put his elbows on his knees and his head in his hands.

"It's a *good* thing, Candy," he said hopelessly.

"I can tell," I replied, but my razor-sharp sarcasm eluded him.

"It's school," he said. "You know I've been working really hard. I wouldn't have pulled an A in algebra without you." He sat up and took my hand, lacing his brown fingers between my skinny, pale ones.

"I know, babe. Congratulations," I said. "Now, what's wrong?"

Carlos put his two hands on my shoulders and looked right into my eyes. I had always thought his eyes were his best feature, but now I realized they were the most beautiful I'd ever seen. They were impossibly dark, so black that his pupils and irises melted together. The whites were as clean and sparkling as his teeth, and any girl would have killed to have his lashes, thick black starbursts against his tan skin.

The words Carlos had said to me once, the words I'd never said back, were rising in my throat and I clamped my lips together hard so they wouldn't escape. No luck.

"I love you," I blurted, just as Carlos blurted, "I'm leaving."

We stared at each other. I put my hand over my mouth.

Carlos blinked. Then a big, stupid grin spread over his stupid face. "You *do* love me," he said, practically yelling. "I knew it!"

I wrenched myself away and stood up, shoving my hands in my pockets. That caused my thumb to erupt in agony. Red seeped through the toilet paper-and-tape bandage, and I ripped it off angrily. "Just shut up," I said, looking at my feet. My sneakers were stupid. Blue and stupid. My jeans were stupid too. So was my stupid thumb, which I held cradled in the hem of my T-shirt. So was the stupid hot flush rising in my face, and the clot of tears gathering in my chest. I was a stupid girl, with a stupid mouth and stupid, stupid feelings.

"Candy," Carlos said gently. "Please, just listen. It's a full scholarship to Tech, and they never start *anybody* midyear—it's a special scholarship, it's an honor, and a lot of money. I could never afford this—it's an amazing opportunity. But I have to take it now. If I don't—"

"Congratulations, Carlos," I said, for the second time that day. "I'm really happy for you."

I turned and walked away, and though he followed me for a few steps, trying to apologize, I ignored him until I was alone, striding down the sidewalk without feelings, a zombie, a dead zombie woman who was somehow still bleeding, a dead zombie woman wearing stupid, stupid shoes.

# A Place Like No Other

I had not been a puppy for many years, but when Black Coat opened the door and I got a whiff of the place, I trembled like one. Even the beagles were silent and still. I had never smelled such a place; the air was suffused with pain and fear, human sweat and excitement, and everywhere, the odor of blood, all the smells running together in the rain. When the Rasp-Voice man crossed the yard toward us, I felt sick and panicked. I remembered his smell and his frightening voice. I remembered the brutal kick he had given me in Bitter Man's basement.

Black Coat stood arguing with Rasp-Voice for a long time, both of them getting wet but not seeming to notice or care. Rasp-Voice was thin and wiry, wearing jeans and a bloodstained sweatshirt. What was odd was that when he came close to the open door of the car, I smelled not the blood of one dog on him, but the blood of dozens, maybe more. He even smelled of cat. And everywhere, a scent filled my nostrils like acid, burning them and making me want to both cower and to run.

"Only one that's any good's the big Aussie shepherd," Rasp-Voice said. He shot the beagles a contemptuous glance. Then he turned back to me, appraising. "And he's already mine," he said firmly. "I bought this dog from a guy who picked 'im up on the road way out in Camarillo. He jumped out my truck when I stopped for a minute. What you tryin' to pull?"

Black Coat shook his head. "I got this dog fair and square. Bought him off a homeless kid over on Clayborne."

"I'm not payin' full price for a dog I already bought once," Rasp-Voice said firmly. "I'll give you somethin' for bringin' him back, but I'm not paying full freight, no way."

I shook, and beneath me the little terrier sensed my fear and began to shake as well.

"They's another dog under the big one you can't see," Black Coat offered. "Another small one. Six dogs in all."

"Only the big un's any good for the ring, the others just for trainin'," Rasp-Voice said again. "Get him out, the big un."

"Boy," Black Coat barked, and the Boy got out, his tears gone. He opened the door and let me smell his hand. For the very first time he let his hand rest on my neck, just for a moment. Then he tugged on the rope and I came out of the car, half jumping, half stumbling.

"He been eatin'?" Rasp-Voice asked, standing a respectful distance from me. I tried to reassure him by lowering myself and whining softly, but instead of petting me or coming closer, Rasp-Voice laughed contemptuously. "I saw this bastard give a helluva bite to a Mexican kid one time."

"Boy," Black Coat called, without taking his eyes off me. "Get them trainers out the car."

The yard where we stood was bare, just mud without grass or plants, although one thin tree stood near the entrance to the alley we'd driven in from. A small, ramshackle house stood at the edge of the yard, and behind that was a garage. The bad smells seemed to come mostly from that garage. It reeked of dog but oddly, I heard no dogs; no barking, no whining, no soft sound of dogs panting in the growing heat.

"He'll fight good if you train him right," Black Coat said. Then, unexpectedly, he gave me a sharp kick in my ribs. It shocked as much as it hurt, and I yelped and whirled on him, showing my teeth before I remembered my wish to befriend these humans.

Both men laughed nervously. "He'll fight," Black Coat repeated.

The Boy had been watching from where he stood by the car. It was hard to read his emotions, which had once been so plain. He no longer smelled of grief or regret or excitement. I thought it was anger I smelled, yet he was calm and steady; no stink of perspiration, no smell of desperation.

Just cold, steady fury, whether with the men or with the dogs, I could not say.

"Hunnerd for the big un," Rasp-Voice was saying. "He's worth two, but I ain't gonna pay twice for the same damn dog. Twenty bucks apiece for the trainers."

Black Coat hesitated, grinned, and extended his hand. "Done."

I barely registered their conversation, or the growing excitement in both men. My attention was fixed on the Boy. I heard him coming up behind me, very softly. I smelled that cold anger on him. I shivered and felt my bowels grow loose. I hoped I would not disgrace myself, but I could not move, with the Boy behind me, clearly wishing me to be still. Rasp-Voice handed money to Black Coat as the Boy's thin fingers worked at the fur around my neck. He slipped the plastic rope from around my neck. Suddenly he slapped my haunch hard, so hard it shocked me even through my thick fur, and yelled, "Run, Big Dog! Run! Run away!"

The men turned as one, Black Coat staring at the Boy in disbelief as Rasp-Voice moved to block the path to the alley, slipping in the mud and cursing furiously. He was no match for me in size, speed, or desperation as I streaked by him. With a sharp shock of regret, I realized the Boy was not running beside me. I was alone, and once more running for my life.

# CHAPTER SEVENTEEN

## *No Power of Any Kind*

My father did not come home for five days. I had a little babysitting cash, but it wasn't enough to get the power turned back on, and I didn't exactly know how to do that anyway. On the third morning, while there was enough sun, I cleaned the kitchen, threw the bits of rotting food out of the fridge and cleaned it, too, and left it propped open so it wouldn't stink. I took all the bedclothes off my father's bed and my own, gathered the towels from the bathroom and kitchen, carried them to the laundromat in two loads, and used a lot of my cash washing and drying everything. I scrubbed the bathroom floor and taped up Mom's china cabinet where the glass had broken. And when I was done, everything was the same. My dad was still gone, my boyfriend was still leaving, the power was still off, and I was still a high school dropout with nowhere to go and nothing much to do.

Carlos kept knocking on the door, but I wouldn't let him in. He tried hanging out in the hall, but I watched out the window and waited until he left for work before I'd come out.

Nights were a little scary. The apartment was very, very dark. Even with the front door chained and bolted, it made me nervous to sleep in my own bed. Instead, I slept on the couch, a candle sparking and guttering in a coffee cup on the table by my head. It was probably not safe, but it felt safer than lying alone in the black night.

On my fourth night alone, someone came tapping when the sun had been down for hours.

"Go away, Carlos," I yelled without getting up off the couch.

Silence for a moment. Then, "Is Mrs. Gomez, Candy. Luisa. Please open the door."

I got up, banged my shin on the coffee table, and let an f-bomb fly. Even with the moon and the light that drifted in beneath the door from the hall-way, it was too dark to see well. I opened the door and yes, it was Mrs. Gomez, but it was also Carlos, looking grim. He put his foot in the door fast before I could slam it closed.

"Candy," Mrs. Gomez said gently. "Come downstairs, please."

I shook my head. "I'm comfortable here, thanks."

She looked up at her nephew, then back to me, and then beyond me into the dark apartment. "How you comfortable? Carlos say you don't have no lights, and your papi's not home. Come downstairs, Candy. I put you with Ana again, like before. Just till Papi come home."

Carlos had not spoken this entire time. I was so embarrassed. Embar-rassed by my lame father, by my stubborn pride, embarrassed to be so clearly and completely unable to cope on my own, embarrassed by my deep and utter longing to follow them downstairs to light, and warmth, and food, and friends.

"No, thank you, Mrs. Gomez," I said firmly. "I promise I'll come down if I need anything, okay? My dad will be back soon."

But I didn't really know if that was true. Carlos was wearing a soft green plaid shirt that I especially loved. He wore it open at the neck with a clean white T-shirt beneath, his strong forearms folded across his chest. His jaw was set in an angry line, but his eyes were soft with worry. I longed to step around Mrs. Gomez, lean against Carlos's chest, and let him wrap his arms around me and keep me safe.

I pushed his foot out of the doorway with my sneaker. "Thank you both very much," I said firmly. And then I shut the door.

# Unbearably Drawn to the Light

I finally stopped running on a dark street without a lot of traffic. I crept cautiously into a small yard and hid behind a bush so I could think. The best thing would be to find the alley where JuJuBee and I had lived with her human. If they were still there, I knew they would welcome me. But I didn't know what Black Coat might have done to JuJuBee's human. At least he hadn't caught JuJuBee, I thought, since he hadn't brought her to the balcony I'd shared with his stolen dogs.

Too many days had passed, and I'd smelled too much, and the constant rain confused odors, and I was very tired. Ever since Black Coat had cracked me on the head with the stick, it had been difficult to think clearly. I'd be resting, or walking, or eating, and then for no reason I would find myself confused, unsure whether I was in Jocelyn's backyard or curled on the rug in Alfie's front hall, and then I'd remember everything and be in the present again. Black Coat and the Boy had fed me well enough, but I'd barely moved in the days spent chained on their balcony, and now my muscles ached from the unaccustomed exercise. My pads were thick and tough from the days walking the streets with JuJuBee and her human, but my eyes didn't seem to see as clearly as they once had, and my ears were definitely not as alert to danger. Only my nose was still sharp, but smelling humans and dogs and cars and all the odors of the street didn't help. The truth was, I had nowhere to go. If I could have found Alfie's old house, or Jared's, I might have gone there, but Black Coat had taken me to a part of the city I didn't know.

The yard where I found myself was modest, but the house looked inviting enough. Two small bicycles were propped by the front step — children! I sighed. Perhaps a child who would ride on my back as Jared had. I could again become a companion and protector. A light burned in one upstairs room, and from a screened window I smelled good cooking—rice, and chicken, and beans, spicy and warm and meaty, and I smelled fresh, cool water and longed for it. I considered creeping up onto the porch and scratching at the door, but some instinct stopped me. Maybe if this family wanted a dog, they would already have one. Yet no dog smell clung to their yard and house, just the pleasing odors of food and garbage and children. Finally I must have fallen asleep, because I woke to the sound of a woman screaming on the steps of the porch a few feet from where I lay.

"Get out of my yard! Get out!" she shrieked, holding a broom out in front of her like a weapon. I sprang to my feet, thinking to protect her from whatever was frightening her, but as I moved toward her, she shrieked again, and I realized that what the woman feared was me.

I stopped, holding very still, trying to show her with my ears and tail that I was no threat. I politely looked away, not wanting my gaze to seem a challenge, but she screamed again and then bent, picked up something from the porch, and threw it at me. A little metal shovel whizzed by my head, barely missing me, and I turned and trotted from the yard. As I emerged onto the street, two big boys walked by, laughing, and their voices sounded warm and good. I thought of walking along beside them, trading my protection for their companionship. But when one of the boys saw me, a mean, angry smell came off of him, and before I could think what to do, he picked up a rock and threw it at me, hard. I darted out of the way but the rock caught me on the left flank and I screamed and turned, not knowing where to run.

The boys laughed again and bumped their fists together in the air, and one said, "Come on, let's get him," and the other bent to pick up more stones. I took off fast, still confused as to how I had become their enemy. They did not seem so different from Alfie and his friends, or from the Boy who had risked Black Coat's anger to set me free and save me from whatever had been planned for me in that blood-soaked garage.

The street that had seemed dark and private the night before was coming alive. Women walked along, holding hands with small children or with older children following behind, some of them carrying umbrellas, others holding folded newspapers or bags over their heads against a light drizzle that made the pavement sparkle. If they saw me, the children looked curious, but the women would stiffen, then move their children cautiously to the other side of the street. But mostly they didn't see me; I kept close to the bushes and trees that offered hiding places, sometimes darting between parked cars if there was nowhere else to escape.

I walked a long time, stopping to rest or to try to get dry beneath a parked car or bush. Once I lapped rainwater from a gutter, but it was tainted with oil and burned my mouth, even as I drank thirstily. Late in the day I passed a yard with a dog chained to a pole. He had no shelter, nowhere to get out of the rain, but he had a bowl brimming with water and another full of rain-soaked kibble. I approached warily and he growled, but unconvincingly. He was shivering and I outweighed him, and besides that, I was not chained.

I drank for a long time, and then I ate, filling my stomach with the rich, soggy kibble, but leaving a bit in the bowl for my host, who now lay with his head on his paws, waiting. I thought of trying to chew through his chain, or perhaps through his leather collar. I imagined us walking the streets together. But when I approached, he stood again, showing his teeth in a weary, life-sick grin, and I moved on, my belly no longer burning, but every leg throbbing, my head pounding, and my flank aching where the stone had hit me, my coat heavy with rain.

At the end of a long, dark block full of ramshackle houses there was one house that was lit up and noisy, even though it was late at night. I crept into the yard, fearful, but unbearably attracted by the light and by that rising, trilling sound humans make when delighted: laughter.

The voices were those of young men and women, not quite children, but not quite adults either. They smelled and sounded as if they might be Alfie's age. I thought of Alfie's father telling his mother, "It's only college," and I wondered if this could be what "college" meant. Could Alfie be here, in this loud, noisy house full of sound and light and smell?

I hid behind a row of garbage cans, listening and waiting, and finally two boys came out of the house, still laughing, punching at each other's arms and speaking so loudly they were nearly shouting. There was no smell of danger from them, just a giddy, happy feeling that made me want to bound toward them, barking. But I knew better, now. I thought about the stone that had bruised my flank and the shovel that had nearly hit my eye.

As the boys came near, I stepped out from behind the cans and stood quietly, wagging my tail to show that I meant no harm.

"Whoa, shit!" one boy yelled, jumping backward almost comically. But the other boy just stood, as if appraising me, and finally held out his hand for me to sniff.

"Relax, Gabe, he's no killer," the boy reassured his friend.

"Jesus, I thought he was a freakin' bear!" the first boy exclaimed. *Bear.* My heart beat fast and I whined deep and low in my throat.

"Easy, boy," the second boy said. "Go on, now, go home."

I whined again and his face grew stern. "Go on. It's dangerous out here for a dog, don't you know that? Go home!"

The boys walked past me, deep in conversation again. After a moment, I fell into step behind them, but when the second boy noticed, he turned and spoke sharply. "Go home!"

I stopped, not sure how to obey. Finally I just stood and watched as the boys disappeared into the black night, the tantalizing sound of their laughter still hanging it the air.

The house was still lit up and noisy, but I was afraid to go too close. I found a spot beneath a small tree and circled until I was comfortable. Then I lay down and slept.

A girl with bare feet approached tentatively, holding a bowl of water. I got up, bones stiff, and stretched, moving slowly and calmly so that she would not be frightened. When she put the bowl down, I moved toward it and drank deeply, lapping up every drop. "You're *so* thirsty," the girl said wonderingly. "I'll get more." She came back a few minutes later, the bowl refilled and sloshing over the sides. She had a loaf of sliced bread tucked under one arm, and as I drank, she put a stack of slices on the ground. It was not what dogs need—the bread was soft and mostly air—but it filled my stomach and I was grateful.

Later that morning, more young men and women stumbled out of the house. Some ignored me, some stopped to offer me a scrap of food, and a few even patted me or scratched around my ears. I thought I might stay there, even if they did not invite me into the house. I could sleep beneath the tree and earn my keep by guarding the house in the early morning, which is when they seemed to sleep.

But soon enough the house was empty, and then a man pushing a big cart arrived and began working around the yard, picking up papers and cans and grumbling. He did not at first seem to notice me. "Damned kids," he said under his breath. "Trash everywhere, like a garbage dump." He stooped to pick up my water bowl, then seemed to consider it, looking around the yard. His eyes landed on me where I waited beneath the little tree.

The man backed away, toward his cart, feeling behind him for something—a broom or a mop. I knew what that meant. I took off before he began to shout.

So it was like that for me for a time—how long, I'm not sure, but there was day upon day of traveling, trotting the sidewalks and streets, darting behind bushes or trash cans. Sometimes I'd be spoken to kindly, or given a meal or allowed to rest beneath a tree or porch. Other times I was run off with angry shouts, or with thrown rocks or sticks. Occasionally I'd meet another dog and we'd travel together for a day or so, but it seemed that two dogs together attracted more attention, and inspired more fear, than one alone. So I stayed mostly by myself, eating and sleeping when I could. One day was like another. Loneliness was like a sad friend that traveled with me everywhere. Sometimes I remembered the sound of Jared's bare feet on the kitchen floor, or Jocelyn's voice calling me to come to supper. Sometimes I remembered Alfie hugging me, or JuJuBee snuggled contentedly against my chest. Sometimes I remembered my real name, *Bear*, and the sound of it on human lips.

## CHAPTER EIGHTEEN

# *Still Candy, But Not So Sweet*

I had just left Julia's house, a crisp twenty-dollar bill in my pocket. I was dreading another night on the couch in the dark, but I was sort of looking forward to it too, in a weird way. It was spooky lying there, but it was calming somehow, with no one to talk to, no way to read or watch TV, nothing to do but think. But when I rounded the corner and looked up at my window, the lights were on. I did a quick Carlos-scan, then let myself into the building and ran up the steps. The door to our apartment was open. My father was in the kitchen, a bag of groceries on the table. He gave me big smile when I came in, then held his arms open wide.

I hesitated. I was not completely glad to see my dad. I was not entirely ready to forgive him. I also wanted to run into his arms and press my face and against his chest and sob.

Guess which won.

The first thing I noticed was that he did not stink of alcohol but smelled like fresh soap and clean clothes. In fact, I recognized the shirt he was wearing—it was one I'd washed and folded at the laundromat during my cleaning spree. He'd gotten the groceries right too. Milk, bread, coffee, cereal, cookies, a bunch of bananas, and a couple packs of sandwich meat. No beer. Go, Dad.

"This is so great," I said, looking around the bright kitchen. "I'm so glad you're home. Did you—did you get a job?"

My father laughed. "There ain't no work out there, Candy-girl. You know that. But there's money to be had if you know how to get it."

That didn't sound good, but I thought it might be better not to ask. My dad had always been a scammer.

"Truth is, I had to spend a couple nights in the clink to get my head straight, but I'm good now."

I felt sick. "You were in *jail*?"

My dad laughed again. "Let's just say your dad had a bit of a disagreement with a bartender, you know?"

I did not know, and did not want to know. "Seriously, Dad? Then where did you get the money to turn the power on and to buy these groceries?"

He grinned as if he'd done some amazing magic trick. "Ask me no questions, I'll tell you no lies," he said grandly. "Candy, sit down. I want to talk to you." He patted the kitchen chair next to his own. "I have not been the best father lately," he said slowly, stumbling over his words. "I know that. I'm gonna do better from now on. No drinking, no trouble. I promise."

I wanted so, so much to believe him.

"Got a dog in the truck," my dad said. "Big one. I think he might be that same dog I sold to Clement, what, four, five months ago?"

Five months before I hadn't even met Carlos yet—he was just a kid on the stoop, studying all the time. I had never taken the Gomez kids swimming or walked them home from school. My dad had never thrown a beer bottle at me or disappeared for four nights. It seemed like so long ago. I remembered the big shepherd-type stray my dad had chained in the basement, the dog that had bitten Carlos when he tried to protect it from Clement's kick. That had been one sad dog, even if he was big and kind of scary looking.

"Well, why don't you do it a favor and let it go," I suggested. "I'd run away from Clement too."

My dad laughed. "I don't blame them dogs either, Candy," he began. Then he must have seen something in my face because he stopped talking.

"What?" I demanded. I felt sick. "What's going on?"

I thought, suddenly and ridiculously, of Cruella De Vil in that Disney movie I'd loved as a kid. She'd wanted Dalmatians to make fur coats, but that was ridiculous. Nobody really wears dog-skin coats. But what else could you do with dogs, really? They could be pets, or guard dogs, or service dogs, like for the blind, I guessed.

My dad's eyes narrowed. "Never mind. I was gonna ask you to run him over there for me, but I can see you're too high and mighty to help your dad out with an errand. Even if I did get the 'lectric turned back on."

*Bravo, Dad. Isn't that your job? Aren't you supposed to take care of me?* But the words echoed only in my head. I didn't dare say them. Or maybe I was just too tired.

"Just before you go getting all long-face over a bunch of stray dogs, think about who pays the rent on this place, and who buys the clothes you wear and the food you eat."

Hmmm. I did as instructed and thought about it. He paid the rent, I guess, assuming he had actually paid it, but of late I'd bought most of my own food and some of his as well. And no one had bought me any clothes in years. I wore my old stuff, my mom's hand-me-downs, and once in a while Julia gave me something or I grabbed a shirt from the giveaway box at Goodwill.

My father got up and slammed out of the room. I heard him on the stairs, and a few moments later, I heard him get into his pickup and roar away.

# A Sad Surprise

I would not have gotten into Bitter Man's truck again; I would have run, or fought. I certainly would not have fallen for his trick of offered food. But I was very tired. Hungry and exhausted, yes, but also weary in a way that went deeper than the gnawing in my belly and the dull ache in my head that sometimes left me confused and forgetful. I'd seen it before, in the chained dog whose food I'd stolen weeks earlier. I'd seen it in dogs brought into the shelter where the blue-haired girl picked who would die and who would live another day. I'd seen it in the injured terrier who had burrowed beneath me in the car on the way to Rasp-Voice's yard, where the Boy had freed me. And now I saw it in myself. I was weary of life and ready to be done.

When Bitter Man offered the bit of bread and meat on the flat of his palm, I did not go to him, but I let him approach. I took the food and sat motionless as he slipped a rope around my neck. When he yanked the rope — harder than necessary — I rose obediently and followed.

We stopped, briefly, at the same building where he had once imprisoned me in the basement, the building where the sad-faced girl had brought me food, where I'd bitten the boy who had tried to protect me from Rasp-Voice's kick. I thought he would chain me in the basement again, but no — I waited in the cab, and after a while he came out again, perspiring and furious. He slammed the car door and took off driving, fast. A horn honked as we sped through an intersection. A woman jumped out of the way as we rounded a corner too quickly. I slid off the seat onto the cramped floor of the truck and stayed there, not caring.

I knew the street we were on; the sight of it, and the bumps and cracks beneath the wheels of the car, and most of all, the stench — that overwhelming odor of anger, fear, and blood. The yard was the same, and the smell. As we pulled in, a chorus of dogs began to bark from the garage. It sounded like a dozen of them, big and small.

It was warmer now, and the ground was covered in a soft, feathery grass instead of being sodden mud as it had been then from the long winter rains. I jumped down from the truck before Bitter Man could pull me, trying to land on my feet, though my joints ached in protest.

Bitter Man dragged me toward the house, and as we crossed the yard, Rasp-Voice came out to meet us, hand extended, a big grin on his weathered face.

"This dog, he keeps coming back to me!" he shouted over the cacophony of dogs barking, and Bitter Man laughed. Rasp-Voice handed Bitter Man a folded bill. "Finder's fee, man," he said heartily. "Thanks."

Bitter Man stuck the bill in his back pocket and started to turn away, but Rasp-Voice stopped him. "Why don' you stay for the fights, man? People start gathering twenty, thirty minutes. We'll pop a couple brews while we wait."

Bitter Man hesitated. A strange, frightening smell came from him. Desire, fear, regret, sorrow. Then he seemed to decide. "Sounds good," he said, following Rasp-Voice across the yard to the garage. With every step we took, the thick uncaring blanket of despair that had come over me grew thinner. I felt anxious and panicked. The smell from the garage was unbearable. As we passed a row of trash cans, I paused, unable to move. I took a deep, painful lungful of air, smelling and tasting the insufferable odor. It was death, and blood, and rot. It was the odor of a dead dog, thrown in the garbage. Not just any dog. It was the rotted carcass of the little terrier that had cowered beneath me on my first trip to Rasp-Voice's yard, before the Boy had set me free.

I sat, lifted my head, and howled, low and deep, at the darkening sky. A dog joined me from inside the garage, then another and another. The men stared for a moment, transfixed. Then they began to laugh.

## CHAPTER NINETEEN

# *Rock Candy*

*Please see me*, the note read. *I can't leave without talking to you.* I'd found the paper tucked under the front door, neatly folded, not addressed or signed, I guess in case my dad found it. But I knew who it was to, and I knew who it was from. "Sure you can," I said aloud, crumpling the note. "Everybody else does." I tossed the note down the stairwell. I didn't have time to think about Carlos. He was a dull throb, like a toothache you can ignore for a while, knowing eventually you'll have to deal with it.

My dad. I'd loved him at one time, and maybe I still did. But he was not the man he'd been when my mother was alive. Even then, he'd had his flaws, of course. He'd been kind of rough, and there'd been times we'd had to do without because he'd spent his paycheck drinking or betting. He'd been careless and irresponsible, but he'd never been cruel.

But a deep suspicion sat in my stomach now, like an undigested meal. I couldn't ignore it and I couldn't get rid of it. I knew what I had to do.

I hadn't been to Clement's in ages, and I don't think I'd ever been after dark. It was as creepy as ever, but Clement wasn't there. A pimply, red-faced white kid who didn't look like he could possibly be legal to work in a liquor store stood behind the counter, reading a dirty magazine and picking his teeth with his fingernail.

"Yeah," he said, in a bored voice, not looking up. Then he did look up, gave me a nasty once-over and an ugly, greedy smile, and tried again. "How can I help you, hot stuff?"

"Where's Clement?" I demanded. "I want to talk to him."

The pimply kid shrugged. "Not here, bae. Won't I do instead?"

"Dude," I said, "it's really important. I need to find Clement. I think my dad is with him."

"He's not here," the boy said again. "Come back tomorrow. He'll be in around eleven—he's always in late the morning after a fight."

"A fight," I said. "You mean, like . . . boxing?"

The boy laughed. "Dogfight." Then it seemed to occur to him that he might be sharing too much information. "Or whatever. Try back tomorrow."

He turned back to his magazine. I just stood there, sick with horror. Dogfighting? Was it possible my father could be mixed up in that? My father, who had patiently taught me to ride a bike, running after me with his hands on the back of the seat until I took off suddenly, on my own? My father who had once taken me to pet store and waited without complaining while I petted every single rabbit, who had helped me coax a cockatiel onto my finger and had stroked its gray feathers as gently as he stroked my hair at night? I pushed from my mind the image of my father throwing a beer bottle at me in anger, of him flashing money and refusing to say where he'd gotten it, of him sprawled drunk on the floor by a pool of vomit. I thought of the big dog he'd once had chained in the basement, the dog that had bitten Carlos, the dog he'd said he'd found again, wandering the streets.

"Give me Clement's address," I demanded. The kid stared at me, slack jawed.

"Tell me where he lives," I repeated, speaking slowly in case he was as dumb as he appeared.

"I can't give you that info," he protested. "I don't even know. I mean, he's over on Sixth, off of Ocean Park, but I don't know—"

But I was already out the door.

# Very Near the End

Blood and fear, anger and blood. Terror, fury, death. And running underneath the animal smells, the dog smells, like a poisonous river running beneath the green earth, human passion: excitement, hunger, thirst, an instinctive lust for animal blood.

The other dogs were in a fury, snarling and snapping against their chains, throwing their muscular bodies against the wire mesh of their cages, showing yellowed teeth broken on bone, ears torn in battle, faces and flanks scarred and healed. I didn't care. I knew then what was to come, and I almost welcomed it. These were dogs like Audrey, as powerful and full of rage. Would they be set upon me in a pack, or would we be expected to fight, one on one, until the end? I welcomed death. I would not fight.

The men were sweat-drenched, their lust fueled by alcohol. They laughed and shouted and groaned as a big red pit was brought out, snarling and snapping against her chain, and an emaciated cat was thrown to her, squalling. It was fast; I believe the cat's fear was worse than its death.

Rasp-Voice unhooked my chain from the bolt on the wall and an excited murmur came from the men gathered around the perimeter of the cement floor, stained with old blood and fresh. I was alone in the center of the room, the din of dog and human voices overwhelming. I felt heat rise in my blood, but I was determined not to fight. Whatever dog they brought to challenge me would have an easy time of it.

They unleashed the red pit, and she charged at me, her teeth still gory with the flesh of the cat. I stood, trembling, despite my wish to die. I let my head hang, but I could still see her coming at me, and then I realized that Black Coat was there, and he had something in a cloth bag, and he was taking it from the bag and throwing it between us, so that we would fight for the right to pull it limb from limb and hear its cry and taste its blood. Another cat, no doubt.

But not a cat.

It landed hard on the cement floor between us and lay, stunned, panting, a mat of fur, but clearly not a cat.

JuJuBee.

# CHAPTER TWENTY

## *Say Good-bye for Me*

Of course, after all that begging to see me, when I needed Carlos, he wasn't home. I turned down Mrs. Gomez's offer of a piece of cake and told her I'd see Carlos the next day.

She looked sad. "Come down early, Candy. Carlos leaves for college tomorrow. My husband will take him to the station at eight-thirty."

Mrs. Gomez brushed a strand of hair off my face and tucked it behind my ear. Her hand on my face shocked me, it was so unexpected and so familiar at the same time. It felt like my mother's hand.

I swallowed hard, trying to push my feelings back under the surface again. I didn't have time to think about whether I'd ever see Carlos again. I felt, suddenly, as if I were emerging from months underground. It was dead night now, but I blinked in the yellow glare of the bare bulb that lit our hallway. I needed to know what my father was up to with Clement, and I wasn't going to let myself glaze over again. I was alive, and it hurt like hell that Carlos was leaving and it hurt like hell that my dad was mixed up in some awful, ugly dogfighting thing with Clement, and possibly didn't even love me anymore, and it hurt that I was a high school dropout and my mom was dead and I didn't have any friends. But the weird thing was, it was a good pain and I wanted to feel it. I wanted to cry. I wanted to scream at my dad and I wanted to throw Carlos's stupid motorcycle book right in his face. I was glad I'd never read it. I didn't care what a stupid Chautauqua was. I wanted to tell my school counselor, Mr. Redmond, and my so-called friend Julia they were adults and they were supposed to help me, not present endless obstacles to every plan I came up with. I wanted to run into the icy ocean and let my tears melt into the waves and let the surf knock me to the floor of the sea and pick me up and then do it again. Most of all

I wanted to see my mother one last time and just tell her how I really felt. Yeah, I love her and I'm gonna miss her forever, but I'm also really, really pissed that she threw her life away, because it didn't have to be like that. She didn't have to smoke like a freakin' chimney and she didn't have to put off going to the doctor until she was already half dead and she didn't have to put up with my dad's drinking. *I am a kid*, I would tell her. *I am a kid and I still need you.* That was one conversation I was never going to have, but it felt good to let the hot red anger flood my body and my brain. It felt good to feel scalding tears run down my face and blood pounding in my wrists and throat.

I wanted to tell the world that I was back, and I was pissed off as hell. But first I had something I needed to do.

"Tell Carlos I said good-bye," I said finally. Mrs. Gomez was still standing in her open doorway. Ana and Vittoria had appeared from nowhere and clung to her hips, and I saw that Ana was crying, for no apparent reason, but I didn't have time to deal with that now.

Then I remembered what I'd thought about Mr. Redmond and Julia and my dad all letting me down, and I thought about how I myself seemed like an adult to someone Ana's age. I knelt down and took her face in my two hands. "Everything is going to be all right, Ana," I told her. I gave her a kiss on the top of her head, and then I rubbed the top of Vittoria's head and blew her a kiss, too, and then I took off down the stairs, running.

## CHAPTER TWENTY-ONE

# Sometimes You're Wrong about People (and Sometimes You Just Wish You Were)

There was an easy bus to Ocean Park and Sixth, but it was a little creepy at night. If I were a normal Los Angeles kid, I'd have had a bike or a skateboard, at least, if not a car, but of course I had none of the above. My dad had left my bike behind when we moved from Studio City, swearing I'd get a better one with his first big paycheck. I did, however, still have the key to my dad's truck on my ring. I fingered it nervously, craning my neck to watch for bus headlights.

I'd waited at the stop less than five minutes when the bus pulled up, and there were so few passengers that we made good time down to Eleventh. "You sure you want to get out here?" the driver asked as the doors opened onto a nearly deserted street. I ignored him and hopped off, walking swiftly toward Ocean, not exactly sure what I'd do when I got there except look for my dad's truck, check on that big dog, and see what Dad and Clement were up to. I had a feeling things were going to be all right, just like I told Vittoria. Maybe I'd misunderstood somehow. As soon as I did my spy work, I could take the bus back home—or if my dad was drunk maybe I could even drive him—and then I could get to bed in time to maybe see Carlos in the morning. I wasn't sure if I wanted to or not, but it felt good to know I had the option.

There was my dad's beat-up Ranger, parked down at the end of one of those cul-de-sacs they put in to try to stop nighttime cruising along residential streets. What this dead end actually did was afford extra parking and privacy to whatever house was there at the end of the block. I figured it was Clement's. There were dozens of cars and trucks parked all around, and although the house was dark, the glow of electric lights spilled from the garage windows and from beneath the door. I heard men's voices and laughter and shouting and excited cursing. To my relief, I did not hear the sounds of dogs.

It was spooky walking down that street. The houses on either side of Clement's were abandoned. One of them had no front steps leading up to the front porch that hung over a dark yard full of rusted junk. The other looked like it had been inhabited more recently; the patio was still neat although the windows were mostly shattered.

The one I figured had to be Clement's was dark, too, but there was definitely a party in the garage. I heard another big shout—lots of men's voices together, excited, sort of the way my dad sounded when he watched a football game on TV. When I was twenty feet from the garage, I did hear a dog then, snarling, and the sound of another panting, but no barking. It was eerie, the way the garage went silent between the collective shouts.

I was afraid. When a soft voice came from eight or ten feet away, I nearly shrieked.

"Don't go in there," the voice said.

I took a deep breath and forced myself to be calm. It was just a boy, maybe twelve or thirteen. It was dark, but I was pretty sure he had been crying, kneeling on the ground by the trash cans. His face was shadowed and nearly unreadable. There was someone else with the boy, lying on the ground. I went closer to him.

The thing on the ground was not a person. It was a big heap of clothes, maybe a fur coat. The boy knelt by it, not touching the pile, just looking at it. I crouched by him and was overcome by a wave of nausea. It was not a pile of clothing; it was a big dog, drenched in so much blood that his coat looked black there in the shadows. Only where his muzzle and paws gleamed in the light from the garage window could I see that the fur beneath the crimson was biscuit colored. He was alive; although his eyes were nearly shut and glazed over, his side moved up and down, slowly but steadily. I was pretty sure it was the Aussie that had once been chained in my basement, the dog I had come looking for.

Now the boy's eyes met mine steadily. "Get out of here," he said in a low, urgent voice. "Girls never come here. It's not for girls."

His chivalry might have been cute if the entire scene had not been so horrifying. From inside the garage, another shout, then clapping and cheering mingled with angry voices. The boy flinched. "Go on. He might be coming out to dump another dead one."

"This one's not dead," I pointed out, but I got the message. I crept back into the yard and pressed myself against a tree, hoping there were no bugs on the trunk. In a moment the garage door opened and a tall man in a black coat came out, saying something over his shoulder into the din of voices. He swung a plastic garbage bag and the boy leapt up fast to catch it.

When he had gone, the boy peeked into the bag and closed it again, fast. I crossed back to him and reached for it, but he shook his head. "Forget it," he said. "Don't look in there."

Something in his voice told me to heed his warning. Instead, I knelt by the big dog on the ground. "It's possible this one could live, if we get him to a vet," I told the boy.

"A vet!" He laughed. "Nobody paying for a vet for this dog. He wouldn't hardly fight. He just stood there like he was gonna let Marjorie rip him to pieces, even when they poked him with the stick and all. And then they threw this bait dog in, and he came alive!"

"A bait dog?" I asked.

The boy nodded. "To bait the real fighting dogs. To get 'em started. But when the guy who lives here, when he threw in that little three-legged bait dog, this big dog, he went crazy. He's supposed to fight Marjorie for the bait dog, to see who gets it, you know? But he got in front of it like he wanted to protect it or something. He wouldn't let Marjorie at it no matter how she came at him. He bit her good, three, four times!"

I looked down at the heap on the ground. "But he still lost the fight."

The boy nodded. "Every dog loses against Marjorie."

I swallowed. "What about the bait dog? The three-legged one. Is it still in there?"

The boy's eyes slid to the bag on the ground.

I ignored a wave of nausea that soured the back of my throat. "I can pick this dog up," I said, "but I'm afraid he's gonna bite me. Dogs do that—they bite when they're scared."

I touched the big dog tentatively. His eye flickered, then closed again.

"I don't think he'll bite you," the boy said softly. "But you can't take him. They'll wonder what happened to him when they leave. Sometimes they like to stop and look at the dead ones, you know?"

"Are there more dogs in there?" I asked the boy, and he nodded.

"Oh, yeah, four fights tonight, and this was only the first one."

I slid my arms under the big dog's body and heaved. If he wanted to bite me, now was the time. My face was not a foot from his red muzzle. But he just groaned as I heaved myself upright. "You won't be here to tell them," I told the boy. "Come with me. I'll help you."

I didn't know how I would help him, but I knew it wasn't right to leave him.

The big dog groaned in my arms. He was too heavy for me to carry for long. I started across the yard, hoping the boy would follow.

"Can you—do you really think you can help him?" he asked. "They always die, the ones they put outside. If they're good enough to live, they keep 'em inside and give 'em medicine and stuff, but the ones they throw out are always dead, or they die right after."

"This dog is not going to die," I said firmly, without believing my own words. What I meant was, he was not going to die lying by a trash can with a bunch of bloodthirsty men ogling his pathetic body on their way out the door. "You can come with me, or you can stay here, but I'm going. Run ahead to that brown truck and see if there's anything like a blanket to lay him on."

The boy hesitated, then ran. When I reached my dad's truck, he had spread some newspapers in the bed for the dog. They wouldn't provide much cushioning, but they would at least soften the jarring of the truck on the street.

My hand on the ignition key was slippery with blood. I felt sick with fear and dread. I had never driven the truck more than just around the block. Now I was taking it at night with nowhere in mind to go. But I knew what I had to do. I beckoned to the boy one more time, but he shook his head and took off running back across the yard to the garage.

The truck started easily and I drove six blocks until I found a mini-mall with a pay phone in the parking lot. I hopped out, pressed 9-1-1, and turned my father in.

## CHAPTER TWENTY-TWO

# *Was I Ever Afraid?*

It was hard to remember why I'd once been so afraid of the basement; it was a warm and safe hideaway from the world now, spiders and all. I didn't know what I was more afraid of—that my father would be arrested and put in jail (again!) or that they'd let him go, and he'd figure out who dropped the dime.

I thought about unloading the big dog and then going back and returning the truck. That way I could find out what happened and also not get arrested for grand theft auto if my dad happened to notice his truck was gone on his way down to central booking. But when I'd finally got the dog out of the truck, down the stairs, and settled onto a pile of old towels, I was just too tired to worry about it. I'd managed to stop the bleeding at his neck by pressing hard on it with a folded rag. He had bites all over his flanks and on one of his back legs, but none of them seemed very deep, though his coat was matted with dried and drying blood. Mostly he seemed exhausted. When I pressed on the neck wound, it had to hurt, but his eyes barely flickered, and he never even whimpered.

"You stay right here," I whispered to the dog. "I'm going to get some stuff from upstairs, and I want you to be really, really, quiet, okay?"

I needn't have worried. Our building was silent.

There was a square of pink paper tacked to the apartment door and for a moment my heart leapt; I thought it might be a note from Carlos. But no, it was a notice from the sheriff requesting that we vacate the premises immediately. I stared at the notice in disbelief. My father had promised me he had paid the rent. We'd gotten three-day notices before and we'd just ignored them. What happens is, if you don't pay your rent, the land-lord puts a note on your door that says "Pay Rent or Quit." Then you've got three days to pay up before the landlord can go to court and get an order to throw you out. But usually they don't want to throw you out and have to hassle with fixing the place up and renting it over again, so they'll give you a few extra days to pay. At least that's the way it had always been before. It had practically been like a joke between my mom and dad. Somehow the money always came through, we paid up, and things would be fine until the next time. But this notice looked serious. It said that if we weren't out in forty-eight hours, the sheriff could lock us out and we'd have to pay to get all our stuff out of storage.

It was embarrassing as hell to leave the note on the door, but if my dad came back, he needed to see it. I went into the apartment and loaded a whole lot of food and a couple of changes of clothes and some blankets into a couple of big reusable grocery bags. I took a long look around the apartment, and then I turned around and went over to the china cabinet and rooted around in the top drawer until I found my mother's wallet. Her driver's license was still in there, and a picture of me as a baby, and a picture of her and my dad looking younger and happier than I'd ever seen them. I stuck the wallet in my back pocket with the lucky sea glass and started to go out again. At the front door, I turned around, went to the fridge, and got a big jug of water we kept in there and a bowl and a glass from the cupboard, and then, without looking around a single time more, I went out, letting the door lock behind me.

⌘ ⌘ ⌘

The dog licked a few drops of water from my fingers, then sighed, long and deep, and let his head drop back down onto the bed I'd made for him.

I wanted to cry. I'd risked a lot to help this dog, and it looked like he was going to die. I wondered if my dad was in jail. I wondered what had happened to the boy who'd been afraid to run away with me. I wondered if the police would even do anything. It had to be illegal to torture animals, didn't it? I thought about what the boy had said, about this big dog fighting to protect a little crippled Chihuahua. Why? What would make a dog care more about another dog than my father cared about me?

I am not a crier. Crying pisses me off. But when I'd spread my own blankets on the floor beside the injured dog, and let my face press lightly against his dirty fur, the tears came. I don't know why. I don't know if I was crying for myself or for him or just for nothing, just 'cause the world is kind of a shitty place.

The dog didn't mind. My tears soaked his fur, and sometime in the night, I must have put my arm around him because that's how it was when I woke up, a thin shaft of sun streaming in the dirty basement window, lighting up the spider webs and cardboard boxes and dusty stacks of junk like it was the Fourth of July.

The first thing I thought of was that the dog was still alive, because his side was heaving in and out, like he was breathing hard. The second thing was that Carlos was gone, because the sun was so bright it had to be a least 10:00 a.m., and Mrs. Gomez had said they were leaving at 8:30.

Good riddance to Carlos, actually, I thought. I hoped he didn't think he'd actually broken my heart or anything. I didn't want anything to ruin his precious time in college.

When I knelt beside the dog with a piece of bread and a mushed up hard-boiled egg, he opened his eyes and gave me a long, steady look. I knew that look. It said, "Thanks, but no thanks."

"Come on, dog," I said. "I know it's not Kal Kan, but it's all we had in the fridge. Try some; it's good." I picked up a little piece of egg and mimed eating it. Then I held out another bite. He sighed and turned his head away. He did not look quite as good in daylight as I'd thought. The cuts and bites on his body were shallow, but there were so many of them that his fur was stiff with blood. One eye was partly shut and his ear hung half off. At least it was no longer bleeding.

"Come on, boy," I told him. "I know you've got to pee. Let's go out."

But when I'd coaxed him to standing, I wanted to weep again. His entire side was matted with dried blood. As if the dog knew I was disappointed, he gave me that sad look again, and then very slowly, he took one step toward me. He leaned his head against my thigh and stood there like that until I let my hand rest on his poor head.

"I am a sad girl," I told him, "and you are a very sad dog. I think that's what I'll call you. Sad Dog." And without a leash or collar, I led him out of the basement toward the stairs.

"Come on, Sad Dog," I coaxed. "Come on, boy. You can make it." But he couldn't. There was something very wrong with his front right paw, and he couldn't put weight on it long enough to get his back legs up the steps. "Okay, I'm gonna pick you up again, okay, boy?"

"Let me help you," a voice behind me said.

Carlos! I whirled around, my heart pounding in my throat and ears. "You're supposed to be gone!" I quickly recovered my composure and said in a much more bored voice, "I mean, it's today, right?"

Carlos looked down at me and started to say something. Then he did a double take. Sad Dog was pressed against my legs, shaking so hard I could feel it, alternately growling and whining but facing Carlos bravely, teeth bared.

"Hey, hey, boy, it's okay," he said gently, sitting down on the top step. "I won't hurt you. I won't hurt *her.*" He put out his hand and the dog stopped growling but still shook.

"I'm trying to get him up the street so he can do his stuff," I said, "but he can't get up the steps. I'm gonna have to carry him."

"Candy," Carlos said, "that dog needs a vet. He looks really bad."

"I can't explain it all right now," I said impatiently. "I—"

But Carlos had butt-scooted down the step, and now the dog was sniffing his hand, very cautiously. I watched him, his glossy hair falling down over his face as he waited patiently until the dog finally allowed him to take its front paw in his hand. There was something about the way Carlos waited, not worried, just calm, and gentle. There was something about the bare nape of his neck. I wanted to turn and run away, as fast as I could, as far as I could.

"Look," Carlos told me. A piece of glass glistened between the dog's black pads. "They do that sometimes, with fighting dogs, to make 'em meaner." My stomach turned at his words.

"Okay, now, I'm trusting you. No biting, okay?" Sad Dog held his head steady, still shaking slightly. Carlos grabbed the shard of glass and yanked it out, fast.

"Good boy, now try again," he said. I wasn't sure if he was speaking to me or to Sad Dog, but I moved up the steps and the dog followed, hesitantly and slowly, but steadily enough. We parked him by a tree and then Carlos turned to me with his arms a little open, as if he expected me to jump into them. I shook my head, refusing to look at him.

"Lemon," Carlos said gently.

"Just go," I said. "Thanks for helping me with the dog. Now you gotta go. Your aunt and uncle must be really pissed."

"Lemon," Carlos said again. "My aunt is upstairs changing my bus ticket and trying not to have a heart attack worrying about you. My uncle is out driving around when he should be at work, looking everywhere for you, because if he doesn't find you, he might as well not come home tonight. They are not pissed, because they know there is no way in a million years I would leave without saying good-bye to you, and there is definitely no way I would leave without knowing where you are and that you are safe, when there is an eviction notice on your front door and we're all pretty sure you never came home last night. And now here you are, covered in dried blood, looking hungry, tired, and pretty pissed off yourself, with a dog that looks like a Mack Truck ran over it, and here I am, waiting for you, arms open wide."

I stared at him. I was pretty sure there was a bubble of snot hanging out of my nose, from when I'd been crying, but I didn't want to wipe it and find out for sure.

"And I will wait as long as it takes," Carlos said, taking one little step closer, "because you are my Chautauqua."

I shook my head. The dog lay down on the sidewalk, eyeing Carlos warily through his reddened eyes.

"I will not leave until I know you are okay," Carlos said quietly. "I will just skip college if you want. Who cares about that scholarship? I care about *you*, Candy. And if I do go, if you and I decide together that you're okay here with me out there, then I'm coming back for you. I love you. I love you forever. When we both graduate, I want to marry you."

I couldn't help it. I laughed out loud. The dog got up painfully and moved to stand against me again. "You can't marry me," I said. "I'm only sixteen. And I'm a high school dropout. And I'm pretty sure I'm about to be homeless." Horribly and humiliatingly, my laugh dried up. My shoulders shook and I could not stop them. I was making a horrible, animal, unappealing noise and no one would ever come back to anyone who made a noise like that. No one would want to marry them. No one would skip college to be with them, I knew that much for sure.

Carlos stopped waiting and stepped toward me. He put his arms around me and rested his head on top of mine. It felt impossibly good to be there pressed against him, even while I was smelling his smell of fresh laundry and soap, knowing I smelled like sweat and morning breath and dog blood.

"You won't come back," I told him. "Nobody ever comes back."

Carlos didn't answer. He let his arms around me be his answer. He let his cheek on the top of my head be his answer. After a long, long time, he led me to the step and we both sat down, the poor old dog inching up as close as he could behind us.

## CHAPTER TWENTY-THREE

# Sad Girl, Sad Dog, Happy Ending(ish)

As it turned out, I was not homeless, because Mr. and Mrs. Gomez invited me to live in Carlos's room for as long as I wanted. Julia invited me too, once word got around. She came to the Gomezes' apartment and practically demanded that I move into their dining room. But Mrs. Gomez did a double whammy on Julia—she gave her the Mexican stare-down at the same time as she offered her a plate of those Mexican wedding cookies, and Julia never had a chance.

I didn't have to pay rent, but I did have to walk Ana and Vittoria and Oscar back and forth from school every day, even when I had morning classes, which was nearly every day. I also had to keep babysitting because I needed money to buy books and personal stuff and especially to send to Carlos, to pay him back for the money he'd lent me to pay the vet.

That wasn't cheap, even at pity rates. The doctor had wanted to keep Sad Dog at the animal hospital on an IV because in addition to having three broken ribs, a dozen dog bites, and a half-healed leg fracture, he was badly dehydrated, and—don't laugh, the doc really said this—clinically depressed. She'd relented when I'd promised to give Sad Dog the ultimate hospital care at home, and I kept my word. Mrs. Gomez wouldn't let me sleep in the basement with Sad Dog, but I visited him first thing in the morning and last thing at night, and in between I walked him, or Mr. Gomez did.

Sad Dog was the best dog I'd ever known. I hadn't known many, of course, not actually being a dog person, but I was pretty sure he was unusual even so. He was incredibly gentle, even when Ana collapsed against him, hugging his sore ribs way too hard, even when Oscar tied a rope around his neck so he could pull a wagon. Sad Dog really liked to walk to the park, although it took him forever, because he limped on his front leg and also because he stopped to smell every single bush, flower, and stranger. I loved to kick off my flip-flops and sit and read with my feet buried in his soft, thick fur. I never had to worry about creeps bothering me. Sad Dog was a very big dog.

But he had to go. He couldn't live in the basement forever, and I couldn't spend all my free time walking him and talking to him, pleasant as that was. See, Julia and Mr. Redmond, between the two of them, they'd cooked up this plan for me to take college classes half-time while finishing my high school credits in the afternoons. I'd actually graduate a year ahead. Not bad for a high school dropout, eh? And Julia and Mrs. Gomez were working on a plan for me to be declared an "emancipated minor," which is like being eighteen when you're not actually eighteen. You can get a job, and rent a place, and all that adulty stuff.

But in the meantime there were classes to take and kids to babysit and Carlos to Skype from the computer lab at school, and I was finally reading *Zen and the Art of Motorcycle Maintenance* because after that horrible wonderful hideous amazing day, I *had* to know what a Chautauqua was. And Sad Dog needed a real home. So I put an ad on Craigslist and turned down the first seven people who responded because they either sounded creepy or flaky or maybe because I just wasn't ready to let him go.

The fourth day the ad ran, I answered the Gomezes' phone and this lady was on the other end and she just sounded really nice. So I invited her to stop by and meet my dog.

CHAPTER TWENTY-FOUR

# *Sometimes They Do Come Back*

She had that kind of weather-beaten prettiness moms get when they're in between being young and being old. There was something about her that seemed sad but also kind; she was a person you'd trust, probably, if you had to trust someone.

She offered Sad Dog a hand to sniff, but instead he sighed deeply, then lay down and put his head on her feet, like he was claiming her. We both laughed, but I'll admit I felt the teeniest bit jealous. "I've been wishing for a big friendly dog like this. Give me some incentive to get up and walk in the morning before it gets too hot out. My other dog's so lazy." She ran her hands all around Sad Dog's neck, working her fingers into the ruff just the way he liked. "What's his name?"

I told her and she broke into a big sunny grin. "I like it," she said. "Sad Dog. It's like a joke, because you can see he's really happy."

Sad Dog's big plumed tail beat against the ground as if he understood her. I let my hand rest on his back, warm beneath the golden sun, and he looked up at me with that big goofy dog grin, his tongue hanging out about a mile. And it was true. He wasn't really a sad dog anymore.

I realized, suddenly, how much I was going to miss him. He wasn't just a dog; he was part of my life. "I had a dog like this once," the woman said. "Years ago. He was an Aussie too — but young, hardly more than a puppy. He was my son's dog. We called him Bear."

Sad Dog whined softly and pushed his head under her hand. She scratched him absently, running her fingers up and down his muzzle and around the base of his ears. Sad Dog had always been friendly to people we met walking or at the park. I trusted him completely with the Gomez kids and Julia's twins; he was that patient and gentle. But I had never seen him take to anyone the way he did to this woman. I hoped he wouldn't overdo it and scare her off with neediness—that can happen, trust me! But she liked him, that much was clear. She stroked his head as we spoke.

"What happened to Bear?" I asked.

"My son—" A shadow of pain crossed her face. "After our son died, my husband—ex, now—he insisted we get rid of everything that had been Jared's. Even the dog. I always regretted letting Bear go." Her eyes drifted away from mine. "I know he found a good home, but still—I think we could have helped each other, Bear and I," she said softly. "We both missed Jared so."

"I lost somebody too," I said, surprising myself. "I lost my mom."

The lady gazed at me steadily, her gray eyes unwavering. "Is it just you and your dad now?"

I shook my head. "My dad—he lives on the street most of the time. He's a . . . a drinker. We've got all our stuff packed up in the basement for when he gets better, you know?" I was suddenly ashamed that I'd confided in her, a stranger, but she met my eyes again with that steady gaze.

"Life can be really hard," the woman said softly. "Nearly impossible. But he might come back to you. He might get well again. People do come back, sometimes."

I shrugged. "Hope so."

Sad Dog whined softly and let his tail thump against the ground again. He looked from me, to the lady, then back to me again, his silky eyebrows lifted into a question.

"Would it be just you and the dogs?" I asked her.

She laughed. "Lord, no! There are six of us, if you don't count the parakeets." She grinned at me. "My husband—my new husband—and me, his three girls—all dog people, Sad Dog, don't you worry! And the beagle is Lucy. Lucy loves other dogs. I don't think she'll make any trouble at all."

Something was stinging my eyes. I blinked and got up. Sad Dog had found a home; I knew it. Now it was my turn. The future stretched out before me like an unmarked road, that frightening, and that full of promise.

Sad Dog got up and followed the lady, as if he'd known her all his life. She jangled her keys in her hand and smacked her thigh with her hand. "Come on, Sad Dog," she called. "Let's go home."

Sad Dog trotted across the room, plumed tail waving joyously. I knew I had to be glad for him, but a tiny, selfish part of me wished he could stay. He stood politely as the lady held the door for him. She whistled, and he followed obediently, a big dumb doggy grin on his weathered face. But just before he left, Sad Dog turned and gave me one long, sweet look from those chocolate eyes, and that look said everything. It said I'd been no great shakes as a dog owner but that he had a lot of faith in me. It said I wasn't so bad, as far as people go. It said—well, I guess it just said thanks.

The lady turned around too, smiling. "Hey," she said, "Candy. Would it bother you a lot if I changed his name?"

# Postscript

**Teenagers struggling with a parent's alcoholism** can find help through Alateen, which is part of Alcoholics Anonymous. The URL is www.al-anon.alateen.org. There are many other local organizations you can find by doing an internet search using the keywords "teenager," "alcoholism," "parent." **If you are a teenager thinking of running away from home,** you can find help and advice at 1-800-RUNAWAY (1-800-786-2929).

**Dogfighting — including being a spectator — is illegal** everywhere in the United States, but how seriously it is taken by the authorities, and how serious the penalties are, vary from place to place. To report dogfighting or animal abuse of any kind, call your local police or sheriff, or find the number of your local animal control agency through directory assistance (411). The ASPCA (www.aspca.org) and the Humane Society (www.humanesociety.org) are successfully combating animal cruelty of all kinds. There are many other local and national organizations you can find by doing an internet search using the key words "dog fighting" or "animal cruelty."